# SAVROLA

# A TALE OF

# IN L

MW01492708

## BY
## WINSTON SPENCER
## CHURCHILL

THIS BOOK IS INSCRIBED
TO
THE OFFICERS
OF THE
IVTH (QUEEN'S OWN) HUSSARS
IN WHOSE COMPANY THE AUTHOR LIVED
FOR FOUR HAPPY YEARS

PREFATORY NOTE

This story was written in 1897, and has already appeared in serial form in Macmillan's Magazine. Since its first reception was not unfriendly, I resolved to publish it as a book, and I now submit it with considerable trepidation to the judgment or clemency of the public.

WINSTON S. CHURCHILL.

CHAPTER I.

AN EVENT OF POLITICAL IMPORTANCE.

There had been a heavy shower of rain, but the sun was already shining through the breaks in the clouds and throwing swiftly changing shadows on the streets, the houses, and the gardens of the city of Laurania. Everything shone wetly in the sunlight: the dust had been laid; the air was cool; the trees looked green and grateful. It was the first rain after the summer heats, and it marked the beginning of that delightful autumn climate which has made the Lauranian capital the home of the artist, the invalid, and the sybarite.

The shower had been heavy, but it had not dispersed the crowds that were gathered in the great square in front of the Parliament House. It was welcome, but it had not altered their anxious and angry looks; it had drenched them without cooling their excitement. Evidently an event of consequence was taking place. The fine building, where the representatives of the people were wont to meet, wore an aspect of sombre importance that the trophies and statues, with which an ancient and an art-loving people had decorated its façade, did not dispel. A squadron of Lancers of the Republican Guard was drawn up at the foot of the great steps, and a considerable body of infantry kept a broad space clear in front of the entrance. Behind the soldiers the people filled in the rest of the picture. They swarmed in the square and the streets leading to it; they had scrambled on to the numerous monuments, which the taste and pride of the Republic had raised to the memory of her ancient heroes, covering them so completely that they looked like mounds of human beings; even the trees contained their occupants, while the windows and often the roofs, of the houses and offices which overlooked the scene were crowded with spectators. It was a great multitude and it vibrated with excitement. Wild passions surged across the throng, as squalls sweep across a stormy sea. Here and there a man, mounting above his fellows, would harangue those whom his voice could reach, and a cheer or a shout was caught up by thousands who had never heard the words but were searching for something to give expression to their feelings.

It was a great day in the history of Laurania. For five long years since the Civil War the people had endured the insult of autocratic rule. The fact that the Government was strong, and the memory of the disorders of the past, had operated powerfully on the minds of the more sober citizens. But from the first there had been murmurs. There were many who had borne arms on the losing side in the long struggle that had ended in the victory of President Antonio Molara. Some had suffered wounds or confiscation; others had undergone imprisonment; many had lost friends and relations, who with their latest breath had enjoined the uncompromising prosecution of the war. The Government had started with implacable enemies, and their rule had been harsh and tyrannical. The ancient constitution to which the citizens were so strongly attached and of which they were so proud, had been subverted. The President, alleging the prevalence of sedition, had declined to invite the people to send their representatives to that chamber which had for many centuries been regarded as the surest bulwark of popular liberties. Thus the discontents increased day by day and year by year: the National party, which had at first consisted only of a few survivors of the beaten side, had swelled into the most numerous and powerful faction in the State; and at last they had found a leader. The agitation proceeded on all sides. The large and turbulent population of the capital were thoroughly devoted to the rising cause. Demonstration had followed demonstration; riot had succeeded riot; even the army showed signs of unrest. At length the President had decided to make concessions. It was announced that on the first of September the electoral writs should be issued and the people should be accorded an opportunity of expressing their wishes and opinions.

This pledge had contented the more peaceable citizens. The extremists, finding themselves in a minority, had altered their tone. The Government, taking advantage of the favourable moment, had arrested several of the more violent leaders. Others, who had fought in the war and had returned from exile to take part in the revolt, fled for their lives across the border. A rigorous search for arms had resulted in important captures. European nations, watching with interested and anxious eyes the political barometer, were convinced that the Government cause was in the ascendant. But meanwhile the people waited, silent and expectant, for the fulfilment of the promise.

At length the day had come. The necessary preparations for summoning the seventy thousand male electors to record their votes had been carried out by the public officials. The President, as the custom prescribed, was in person to sign the necessary writ of summons to the faithful citizens. Warrants for election would be forwarded to the various electoral divisions in the city and the provinces, and those who were by the ancient law entitled to the franchise would give their verdict on the conduct of him whom the Populists in bitter hatred had called the Dictator.

It was for this moment that the crowd was waiting. Though cheers from time to time arose, they waited for the most part in silence. Even when the President had passed on his way to the Senate, they had foreborne to hoot; in their eyes he was virtually abdicating, and that made amends for all. The time-honoured observances, the long-loved

2

rights would be restored, and once more democratic government would be triumphant in Laurania.

Suddenly, at the top of the steps in the full view of the people, a young man appeared, his dress disordered and his face crimson with excitement. It was Moret, one of the Civic Council. He was immediately recognised by the populace, and a great cheer arose. Many who could not see him took up the shout, which re-echoed through the square, the expression of a nation's satisfaction. He gesticulated vehemently, but his words, if he spoke at all, were lost in the tumult. Another man, an usher, followed him out hurriedly, put his hand on his shoulder, appeared to speak with earnestness, and drew him back into the shadow of the entrance. The crowd still cheered.

A third figure issued from the door, an old man in the robes of municipal office. He walked, or rather tottered feebly down the steps to a carriage, which had drawn up to meet him. Again there were cheers. "Godoy! Godoy! Bravo, Godoy! Champion of the People! Hurrah, hurrah!"

It was the Mayor, one of the strongest and most reputable members of the party of Reform. He entered his carriage and drove through the open space, maintained by the soldiery, into the crowd, which, still cheering, gave way with respect.

The carriage was open and it was evident that the old man was painfully moved. His face was pale, his mouth puckered into an expression of grief and anger, his whole frame shaken with suppressed emotion. The crowd had greeted him with applause, but, quick to notice, were struck by his altered appearance and woeful looks. They crowded round the carriage crying: "What has happened? Is all well? Speak, Godoy, speak!" But he would have none of them, and quivering with agitation bade his coachman drive the faster. The people gave way slowly, sullenly, thoughtfully, as men who make momentous resolutions. Something had happened, untoward, unforeseen, unwelcome; what this was, they were anxious to know.

And then began a period of wild rumour. The President had refused to sign the writs; he had committed suicide; the troops had been ordered to fire; the elections would not take place, after all; Savrola had been arrested,—seized in the very Senate, said one, murdered added another. The noise of the multitude changed into a dull dissonant hum of rising anger.

At last the answer came. There was a house, overlooking the square, which was separated from the Chamber of Representatives only by a narrow street, and this street had been kept clear for traffic by the troops. On the balcony of this house the young man, Moret, the Civic Councillor, now reappeared, and his coming was the signal for a storm of wild, anxious cries from the vast concourse. He held up his hand for silence and after some moments his words became audible to those nearest. "You are betrayed—a cruel fraud—the hopes we had cherished are dashed to the ground—all has been done in vain— Cheated! cheated! cheated!" The broken fragments of his oratory reached far into the mass of excited humanity, and then he shouted a sentence, which was heard by thousands and repeated by thousands more. "The register of citizenship has been mutilated, and the names of more than half the electors have been erased. To your tents, oh people of Laurania!"

3

For an instant there was silence, and then a great sob of fury, of disappointment, and of resolve arose from the multitude.

At this moment the presidential carriage, with its four horses, its postilions in the Republican livery, and an escort of Lancers, moved forward to the foot of the steps, as there emerged from the Parliament House a remarkable figure. He wore the splendid blue and white uniform of a general of the Lauranian Army; his breast glittered with medals and orders; his keen strong features were composed. He paused for a moment before descending to his carriage, as if to give the mob an opportunity to hiss and hoot to their content, and appeared to talk unconcernedly with his companion, Señor Louvet, the Minister of the Interior. He pointed once or twice towards the surging masses, and then walked slowly down the steps. Louvet had intended to accompany him, but he heard the roar of the crowd and remembered that he had some business to attend to in the Senate that could not be delayed; the other went on alone. The soldiers presented arms. A howl of fury arose from the people. A mounted officer, who sat his horse unmoved, an inexorable machine, turned to a subordinate with an order. Several companies of foot-soldiers began defiling from the side street on the right of the Chamber, and drawing up in line in the open space which was now partly invaded by the mob.

The President entered his carriage which, preceded by an entire troop of Lancers, immediately started at a trot. So soon as the carriage reached the edge of the open space, a rush was made by the crowd. The escort closed up; "Fall back there!" shouted an officer, but he was unheeded. "Will you move, or must we move you?" said a gruffer voice. Yet the mob gave not an inch. The danger was imminent. "Cheat! Traitor! Liar! Tyrant!" they shouted, with many other expressions too coarse to be recorded. "Give us back our rights—you, who have stolen them!"

And then some one at the back of the crowd fired a revolver into the air. The effect was electrical. The Lancers dropped their points and sprang forward. Shouts of terror and fury arose on all sides. The populace fled before the cavalry; some fell on the ground and were trampled to death; some were knocked down and injured by the horses; a few were speared by the soldiers. It was a horrible scene. Those behind threw stones, and some fired random pistol shots. The President remained unmoved. Erect and unflinching he gazed on the tumult as men gaze at a race about which they have not betted. His hat was knocked off, and a trickle of blood down his cheek showed where a stone had struck. For some moments the issue seemed doubtful. The crowd might storm the carriage and then,—to be torn to pieces by a rabble! There were other and more pleasant deaths. But the discipline of the troops overcame all obstacles, the bearing of the man appeared to cow his enemies, and the crowd fell back, still hooting and shouting.

Meanwhile the officer commanding the infantry by the Parliament House had been alarmed by the rushes of the mob, which he could see were directed at the President's carriage. He determined to create a diversion. "We shall have to fire on them," he said to the Major who was beside him.

"Excellent," replied that officer; "it will enable us to conclude those experiments in penetration, which we have been trying with the soft-nosed bullet. A very valuable experiment, Sir," and then turning to the soldiers he issued several orders. "A very valuable experiment," he repeated.

"Somewhat expensive," said the Colonel dryly; "and half a company will be enough, Major."

There was a rattle of breech-blocks as the rifles were loaded. The people immediately in front of the troops struggled madly to escape the impending volley. One man, a man in a straw hat, kept his head. He rushed forward. "For God's sake don't fire!" he cried. "Have mercy! We will disperse."

There was a moment's pause, a sharp order and a loud explosion, followed by screams. The man in the straw hat bent backwards and fell on the ground; other figures also subsided and lay still in curiously twisted postures. Every one else except the soldiers fled; fortunately there were many exits to the square, and in a few minutes it was almost deserted. The President's carriage made its way through the flying crowd to the gates of the palace, which were guarded by more soldiers, and passed through in safety.

All was now over. The spirit of the mob was broken and the wide expanse of Constitution Square was soon nearly empty. Forty bodies and some expended cartridges lay on the ground. Both had played their part in the history of human developement and passed out of the considerations of living men. Nevertheless the soldiers picked up the empty cases, and presently some police came with carts and took the other things away, and all was quiet again in Laurania.

CHAPTER II.

THE HEAD OF THE STATE.

The carriage and its escort passed the ancient gateway and driving through a wide courtyard drew up at the entrance of the palace. The President alighted. He fully appreciated the importance of retaining the good will and support of the army, and immediately walked up to the officer who commanded the Lancers. "None of your men hurt, I trust," he said.

"Nothing serious, General," replied the subaltern.

"You handled your troop with great judgment and courage. It shall be remembered. But it is easy to lead brave men; they shall not be forgotten. Ah, Colonel, you are quite right to come to me. I anticipated some trouble with the disaffected classes, so soon as it became known that we were still determined to maintain law and order in the State." These last words were spoken to a dark, bronzed man who had hurriedly entered the courtyard by a side gate. Colonel Sorrento, for such was the newcomer's name, was the military chief of the Police. Besides filling this important office, he discharged the duties of War-Minister to the Republic. The combination enabled the civil power to be supplemented by the military with great and convenient promptitude, whenever it was necessary or desirable to take strong measures. The arrangement was well suited to the times. Usually Sorrento was calm and serene. He had seen many engagements and much war of the type which knows no quarter, had been several times wounded, and was regarded as a brave and callous man. But there is something appalling in the concentrated fury of a mob, and the Colonel's manner betrayed the fact that he was not quite proof against it.

"Are you wounded, Sir?" he asked, catching sight of the President's face.

"It is nothing,—a stone; but they were very violent. Some one had roused them; I had hoped to get away before the news was known. Who was it spoke to them?"

"Moret, the Civic Councillor, from the balcony of the hotel. A very dangerous man! He told them they were betrayed."

"Betrayed? What audacity! Surely such language would come within the 20th Section of the Constitution: Inciting to violence against the person of the Head of the State by misrepresentation or otherwise." The President was well versed in those clauses of the public law which were intended to strengthen the hands of the Executive. "Have him arrested, Sorrento. We cannot allow the majesty of Government to be insulted with impunity,—or stay, perhaps it would be wiser to be magnanimous now that the matter is settled. I do not want a State prosecution just at present." Then he added in a louder voice: "This young officer, Colonel, discharged his duty with great determination,—a most excellent soldier. Please see that a note is made of it. Promotion should always go by merit, not by age, for services and not for service. We will not forget your behaviour, young man."

He ascended the steps and entered the hall of the palace, leaving the subaltern, a boy of twenty-two, flushed with pleasure and excitement, to build high hopes of future command and success.

The hall was spacious and well-proportioned. It was decorated in the purest style of the Lauranian Republic, the arms of which were everywhere displayed. The pillars were of ancient marble and by their size and colour attested the wealth and magnificence of former days. The tessellated pavement presented a pleasing pattern. Elaborate mosaics on the walls depicted scenes from the national history: the foundation of the city; the peace of 1370; the reception of the envoys of the Great Mogul: the victory of Brota; the death of Saldanho, that austere patriot, who died rather than submit to a technical violation of the Constitution. And then coming down to later years, the walls showed the building of the Parliament House: the naval victory of Cape Cheronta, and finally the conclusion of the Civil War in 1883. On either side of the hall, in a deep alcove, a bronze fountain, playing amid surrounding palms and ferns, imparted a feeling of refreshing coolness to the eye and ear. Facing the entrance was a broad staircase, leading to the state rooms whose doors were concealed by crimson curtains.

A woman stood at the top of the stairs. Her hands rested on the marble balustrade; her white dress contrasted with the bright-coloured curtains behind her. She was very

6

beautiful, but her face wore an expression of alarm and anxiety. Woman-like she asked three questions at once. "What has happened, Antonio? Have the people risen? Why have they been firing?" She paused timidly at the head of the stairs, as if fearing to descend.

"All is well," replied the President in his official manner. "Some of the disaffected have rioted, but the Colonel here has taken every precaution and order reigns once more, dearest." Then turning to Sorrento, he went on: "It is possible that the disturbances may be renewed. The troops should be confined to barracks and you may give them an extra day's pay to drink the health of the Republic. Double the Guards and you had better have the streets patrolled to-night. In case anything happens, you will find me here. Good-night, Colonel." He walked up a few steps, and the War-Minister, bowing gravely, turned and departed.

The woman came down the stairs and they met midway. He took both her hands in his and smiled affectionately; she, standing one step above him, bent forward and kissed him. It was an amiable, though formal, salutation.

"Well," he said, "we have got through to-day all right, my dear; but how long it can go on, I do not know; the revolutionaries seem to get stronger every day. It was a very dangerous moment just now in the square; but is over for the present."

"I have passed an anxious hour," she said, and then, catching sight for the first time of his bruised forehead, she started. "But you are wounded."

"It is nothing," said the President. "They threw stones; now, we used bullets; they are better arguments."

"What happened at the Senate?"

"I had expected trouble, you know. I told them in my speech that, in spite of the unsettled state of affairs, we had decided to restore the ancient Constitution of the Republic, but that it had been necessary to purge the register of the disaffected and rebellious. The Mayor took it out of the box and they scrambled over each other to look at the total electorates for the divisions. When they saw how much they were reduced they were very angry. Godoy was speechless; he is a fool, that man. Louvet told them that it must be taken as an instalment, and that as things got more settled the franchise would be extended; but they howled with fury. Indeed, had it not been for the ushers and for a few men of the Guard, I believe they would have assaulted me there and then in the very Chamber itself. Moret shook his fist at me,—ridiculous young ass—and rushed out to harangue the mob."

"And Savrola?"

"Oh, Savrola,—he was quite calm; he laughed when he saw the register. 'It is only a question of a few months,' he said; 'I wonder you think it worth while.' I told him that I did not understand him, but he spoke the truth for all that;" and then, taking his wife's hand in his, he climbed the stairs slowly and thoughtfully.

7

But there is little rest for a public man in times of civil disturbance. No sooner had Molara reached the top of the stairs and entered the reception-room, than a man advanced to meet him from a door at the far end. He was small, dark, and very ugly, with a face wrinkled with age and an indoor life. Its pallor showed all the more by contrast with his hair and short moustache, both of which were of that purple blackness to which Nature is unable to attain. In his hand he carried a large bundle of papers, carefully disposed into departments by his long and delicate fingers. It was the Private Secretary.

"What is it, Miguel?" asked the President; "you have some papers for me?"

"Yes, Sir; a few minutes will suffice. You have had an exciting day; I rejoice it has terminated successfully."

"It has not been devoid of interest," said Molara, wearily. "What have you got for me?"

"Several foreign despatches. Great Britain has sent a note about the Sphere of Influence to the south of the African Colony, to which the Foreign Minister has drafted a reply."

"Ah! these English,—how grasping, how domineering! But we must be firm. I will maintain the territories of the Republic against all enemies, internal or external. We cannot send armies, but, thank God, we can write despatches. Is it strong enough?"

"Your Excellency need have no fears. We have vindicated our rights most emphatically; it will be a great moral victory."

"I hope we shall get material as well as moral good out of it. The country is rich; there is paying gold; that explains the note. Of course we must reply severely. What else?"

"There are some papers relating to the army, commissions and promotions, Sir," said Miguel, fingering one particular bundle of his papers, the bundle that lay between his first and second fingers. "Those sentences for confirmation, a draft of Morgon's Budget for information and opinion, and one or two minor matters."

"H'm, a long business! Very well, I will come and see to it. Dearest, you know how pressed I am. We shall meet to-night at the dinner. Have all the Ministers accepted?"

"All but Louvet, Antonio. He is detained by business."

"Business, pooh! He is afraid of the streets at night. What a thing it is to be a coward! Thus he misses a good dinner. At eight then, Lucile." And with a quick and decided step he passed through the small door of the private office followed by the Secretary.

Madame Antonio Molara remained standing for a moment in the great reception-room. Then she walked to the window and stepped out on to the balcony. The scene which stretched before her was one of surpassing beauty. The palace stood upon high ground commanding a wide view of the city and the harbour. The sun was low on the horizon, but the walls of the houses still stood out in glaring white. The red and blue tiled roofs were relieved by frequent gardens and squares whose green and graceful palms soothed and gratified the eye. To the north the great pile of the Senate House and Parliament buildings loomed up majestic and imposing. Westward lay the harbour with its shipping and protecting forts. A few warships floated in the roads, and many white-sailed smacks dotted the waters of the Mediterranean Sea, which had already begun to change their blue for the more gorgeous colours of sunset.

As she stood there in the clear light of the autumn evening, she looked divinely beautiful. She had arrived at that age of life, when to the attractions of a maiden's beauty are added those of a woman's wit. Her perfect features were the mirror of her mind, and displayed with every emotion and every mood that vivacity of expression which is the greatest of woman's charms. Her tall figure was instinct with grace, and the almost classic dress she wore enhanced her beauty and harmonised with her surroundings.

Something in her face suggested a wistful aspiration. Lucile had married Antonio Molara nearly five years before, when he was in the height and vigour of his power. Her family had been among the stoutest supporters of his cause, and her father and brother had lost their lives on the battlefield of Sorato. Her mother, broken down by calamity and sorrow, lived only to commend her daughter to the care of their most powerful friend, the general who had saved the State and would now rule it. He had accepted the task at first from a feeling of obligation to those who had followed his star so faithfully, but afterwards from other motives. Before a month had passed he fell in love with the beautiful girl whom Fortune had led to him. She admired his courage, his energy, and his resource; the splendours of the office that he filled were not without their influence; he offered her wealth and position,—almost a throne; and besides he was a fine figure of a man. She was twenty-three when they married. For many months her life had been a busy one. Receptions, balls, and parties had filled the winter season with the unremitting labour of entertaining. Foreign princes had paid her homage, not only as the loveliest woman in Europe, but also as a great political figure. Her salon was crowded with the most famous men from every country. Statesmen, soldiers, poets, and men of science had worshipped at the shrine. She had mixed in matters of State. Suave and courtly ambassadors had thrown out delicate hints, and she had replied with unofficial answers. Plenipotentiaries had explained the details of treaties and protocols, with remarkable elaboration, for her benefit. Philanthropists had argued, urged, and expounded their views or whims. Every one talked to her of public business. Even her maid had approached her with an application for the advancement of her brother, a clerk in the Post Office; and every one had admired her until admiration itself, the most delicious drink that a woman tastes, became insipid.

But even during the first few years there had been something wanting. What it was Lucile had never been able to guess. Her husband was affectionate and such time as he could spare from public matters was at her service. Of late things had been less bright. The agitation of the country, the rising forces of Democracy, added to the already heavy business of the Republic, had taxed the President's time and energies to the full. Hard lines had come into his face, lines of work and anxiety, and sometimes she had caught a look of awful weariness, as of one who toils and yet foresees that his labour will be vain. He saw her less frequently, and in those short intervals talked more and more of business and politics.

9

A feeling of unrest seemed to pervade the capital. The season, which had just begun, had opened badly. Many of the great families had remained in their summer residences on the slopes of the mountains, though the plains were already cool and green; others had kept to their own houses in the city, and only the most formal entertainments at the palace had been attended. As the outlook became more threatening it seemed that she was able to help him less. Passions were being roused that blinded the eyes to beauty and dulled the mind to charm. She was still a queen, but her subjects were sullen and inattentive. What could she do to help him, now that he was so hard pressed? The thought of abdication was odious to her, as to every woman. Must she remain directing the ceremonies of the Court after the brilliancy had died out, while enemies were working night and day to overturn all that she was attached to?

"Can I do nothing, nothing?" she murmured. "Have I played my part? Is the best of life over?" and then, with a hot wave of petulant resolve, "I will do it,—but what?"

The question remained unanswered; the edge of the sun dipped beneath the horizon and at the end of the military mole, from the shapeless mound of earth that marked the protecting battery of the harbour, sprang a puff of smoke. It was the evening gun, and the sound of the report, floating faintly up to her, interrupted the unpleasing reflections which had filled her thoughts; but they left a memory behind. She turned with a sigh and re-entered the palace; gradually the daylight died away and it became night.

CHAPTER III.

THE MAN OF THE MULTITUDE.

Dismay and bitter anger filled the city. The news of the fusilade spread fast and far, and, as is usual on such occasions, its effects were greatly exaggerated. But the police precautions were well conceived and ably carried out. Nothing like a crowd was allowed to gather, and the constant patrolling of the streets prevented the building of barricades. The aspect of the Republican Guard was moreover so formidable that, whatever the citizens might feel, they found it discreet to display an acquiescent, and in some cases even a contented demeanour.

With the leaders of the Popular party it was however different. They immediately assembled at the official residence of the Mayor, and a furious discussion ensued. In the hall of the Mayoralty an emergency meeting was held, at which all the power of the party was represented. Moret, the Civic Councillor and former editor of the suppressed TRUMPET CALL, was much cheered as he entered the room. His speech had appealed to many, and the Lauranians were always ready to applaud a daring act. Besides, every one was agitated by the recent riot and was eager to do something. The Labour delegates were particularly angry. Working-men, assembled in constitutional manner to express their grievances, had been shot down by a hireling soldiery,—massacred was the word most

10

generally used. Vengeance must be taken; but how? The wildest schemes were suggested. Moret, always for bold counsels, was for sallying into the streets and rousing the people to arms; they would burn the palace, execute the tyrant, and restore the liberties of the land. Godoy, old and cautious, strongly opposed the suggestion, though indeed no particular eagerness was shown to adopt it. He advocated a calm and dignified attitude of reproach and censure, which would appeal to the comity of nations and vindicate the justice of their cause. Others took up the argument. Renos, the barrister, was for what he called constitutional methods. They should form themselves into a Committee of Public Safety; they should appoint the proper officers of State (including of course an Attorney-General), and decree the deposition of the President for violation of the fundamental principles contained in the preamble of the Declaration of National Rights. He proceeded to dilate upon the legal points involved, until interrupted by several members who were anxious to offer their own remarks.

Several resolutions were passed. It was agreed that the President had forfeited the confidence of the citizens, and he was forthwith called upon to resign his office and submit himself to the Courts of Law. It was also agreed that the army had deserved ill of the Republic. It was resolved to prosecute at civil law the soldiers who had fired on the people, and a vote of sympathy was carried in favour of the relations of the killed and wounded, or martyrs as they were called.

This scene of impotence and futility was ended by the entrance of the remarkable man who had raised a party from the dust, and had led them from one success to another until it had seemed that the victory was won. Silence fell upon the assemblage; some stood up in respect; everyone wondered what he would say. How would he bear the crushing defeat that had fallen upon them? Would he despair of the movement? Would he be angry or sad or cynical? Above all, what course would he propose?

He walked to the end of the long table around which the members were grouped, and sat down deliberately. Then he looked round the room, with a face as calm and serene as ever. In that scene of confusion and indecision he looked magnificent. His very presence imparted a feeling of confidence to his followers. His high and ample forehead might have contained the answer to every question; his determined composure seemed equal to the utmost stroke of Fate.

After a moment's pause, invited by the silence, he rose. His words were studiously moderate. It had been a disappointment to him, he said, to find that the registers had been mutilated. The ultimate success was deferred, but it was only deferred. He had waited before coming to the Mayoralty to make a few calculations. They were necessarily rough and hurried, but he thought they were approximately correct. The President, it was true, would have a majority in the forthcoming Parliament, and a substantial majority; but they would win certain seats, in spite of the restricted electorate; about fifty, he thought, in a house of three hundred. Smaller minorities than that had overthrown more powerful Governments. Every day added to their strength; every day increased the hatred of the Dictator. Besides, there were other alternatives than constitutional procedure,—and at these words some set their teeth and looked at each other in deep significance—but for the present they must wait; and they could afford to wait, for the prize was worth winning. It was the most precious possession in the world,—liberty. He sat down amid brighter faces and calmer minds. The deliberations were resumed. It was decided to relieve, out of the general funds of the party, those who were in poverty through the massacre of their relations; that would increase their popularity with the working classes, and might win the sympathy of foreign nations. A deputation should wait on the President to express the grief of the citizens at the mutilation of their ancient register, and to beg that he would restore their franchises. It should also demand the punishment of the officers who had fired on the people, and should acquaint the President with the alarm and indignation of the city. Savrola, Godoy, and Renos were named as the members of the deputation, and the Reform Committee then dispersed quietly.

Moret lingered till the end and approached Savrola. He was surprised that he had not been suggested as a member of the deputation. He knew his leader much better than Renos, a pedantic lawyer who made few friends: he had followed Savrola from the beginning with blind enthusiasm and devotion; and he now felt hurt that he should be passed over like this.

"It has been a bad day for us," he said tentatively; and then as Savrola did not reply, he continued, "Who would have thought they would have dared to trick us?"

"It has been a very bad day,—for you," replied Savrola thoughtfully.

"For me? Why, what do you mean?"

"Have you reflected that you have forty human lives to answer for? Your speech was useless,—what good could it do? Their blood is on your head. The people too are cowed. Much harm has been done; it is your fault."

"My fault! I was furious,—he cheated us,—I thought only of revolt. I never dreamed you would sit down tamely like this. That devil should be killed now, at once,— before more mischief happens."

"Look here, Moret: I am as young as you; I feel as acutely; I am full of enthusiasm. I, too, hate Molara more than is wise or philosophic; but I contain myself, when nothing is to be gained by giving way. Now mark my words. Either you learn to do so, or you can go your ways, for I will have none of you,—politically, that is,—as a friend, it is different."

He sat down and began to write a letter, while Moret, pale with that mortification which is made up of anger and self-reproach, and quivering under his rebuke, left the room in haste.

Savrola remained. There was much business to do that evening; letters had to be written and read, the tone of the leading-articles in the Democratic Press explained, and many other matters decided. The machinery of a great party, and still more of a great conspiracy, needed careful and constant attention. It was nine o'clock before he finished.

"Well, good-night, Godoy," he said to the Major; "we shall have another busy day to-morrow. We must contrive to frighten the Dictator. Let me know at what time he will give audience."

12

At the door of the Mayoralty he called a hackney-coach, a conveyance which neither the dulness of the social season nor the excitement of political affairs could restrain from its customary occupation. After a short drive he arrived at a small though not inelegant house, for he was a man of means, in the most fashionable quarter of the town. An old woman opened the door to his knock. She looked rejoiced to see him.

"La," she said, "I have had a fearful time with you away, and all this shooting and noise. But the afternoons are chilly now and you should have had your coat; I fear you will have a cold to-morrow."

"It is all right, Bettine," he answered kindly; "I have a good chest, thanks to your care; but I am very tired. Send me some soup to my room; I will not dine to-night."

He went upstairs, while she bustled off to get him the best dinner she could improvise. The apartments he lived in were on the second storey—a bedroom, a bathroom, and a study. They were small, but full of all that taste and luxury could devise and affection and industry preserve. A broad writing-table occupied the place of honour. It was arranged so that the light fell conveniently to the hand and head. A large bronze inkstand formed the centrepiece, with a voluminous blotting-book of simple manufacture spread open before it. The rest of the table was occupied by papers on files. The floor, in spite of the ample waste-paper basket, was littered with scraps. It was the writing-table of a public man.

The room was lit by electric light in portable shaded lamps. The walls were covered with shelves, filled with well-used volumes. To that Pantheon of Literature none were admitted till they had been read and valued. It was a various library: the philosophy of Schopenhauer divided Kant from Hegel, who jostled the Memoirs of St. Simon and the latest French novel; RASSELAS and LA CURÉE lay side by side; eight substantial volumes of Gibbon's famous History were not perhaps inappropriately prolonged by a fine edition of the DECAMERON; the ORIGIN OF SPECIES rested by the side of a black-letter Bible; THE REPUBLIC maintained an equilibrium with VANITY FAIR and the HISTORY OF EUROPEAN MORALS. A volume of Macaulay's Essays lay on the writing-table itself; it was open, and that sublime passage whereby the genius of one man has immortalised the genius of another was marked in pencil. And history, while for the warning of vehement, high, and daring natures, she notes his many errors, will yet deliberately pronounce that among the eminent men whose bones lie near his, scarcely one has left a more stainless, and none a more splendid name.

A half-empty box of cigarettes stood on a small table near a low leathern armchair, and by its side lay a heavy army-revolver, against the barrel of which the ashes of many cigarettes had been removed. In the corner of the room stood a small but exquisite Capitoline Venus, the cold chastity of its colour reproaching the allurements of its form. It was the chamber of a philosopher, but of no frigid, academic recluse; it was the chamber of a man, a human man, who appreciated all earthly pleasures, appraised them at their proper worth, enjoyed, and despised them.

There were still some papers and telegrams lying unopened on the table, but Savrola was tired; they could, or at any rate should wait till the morning. He dropped into his chair. Yes, it had been a long day, and a gloomy day. He was a young man, only thirty-

13

two, but already he felt the effects of work and worry. His nervous temperament could not fail to be excited by the vivid scenes through which he had lately passed, and the repression of his emotion only heated the inward fire. Was it worth it? The struggle, the labour, the constant rush of affairs, the sacrifice of so many things that make life easy, or pleasant—for what? A people's good! That, he could not disguise from himself, was rather the direction than the cause of his efforts. Ambition was the motive force, and he was powerless to resist it. He could appreciate the delights of an artist, a life devoted to the search for beauty, or of sport, the keenest pleasure that leaves no sting behind. To live in dreamy quiet and philosophic calm in some beautiful garden, far from the noise of men and with every diversion that art and intellect could suggest, was, he felt, a more agreeable picture. And yet he knew that he could not endure it. 'Vehement, high, and daring' was his cast of mind. The life he lived was the only one he could ever live; he must go on to the end. The end comes often early to such men, whose spirits are so wrought that they know rest only in action, contentment in danger, and in confusion find their only peace.

His thoughts were interrupted by the entrance of the old woman with a tray. He was tired, but the decencies of life had to be observed; he rose, and passed into the inner room to change his clothes and make his toilet. When he returned, the table was laid; the soup he had asked for had been expanded by the care of his house-keeper into a more elaborate meal. She waited on him, plying him the while with questions and watching his appetite with anxious pleasure. She had nursed him from his birth up with a devotion and care which knew no break. It is a strange thing, the love of these women. Perhaps it is the only disinterested affection in the world. The mother loves her child; that is material nature. The youth loves his sweetheart; that too may be explained. The dog loves his master; he feeds him; a man loves his friend; he has stood by him perhaps at doubtful moments. In all there are reasons; but the love of a foster-mother for her charge appears absolutely irrational. It is one of the few proofs, not to be explained even by the association of ideas, that the nature of mankind is superior to mere utilitarianism, and that his destinies are high.

The light and frugal supper finished, the old woman departed with the plates, and he fell to his musings again. Several difficult affairs impended in the future, about the conduct of which he was doubtful. He dismissed them from his mind; why should he be always oppressed with matters of fact? What of the night? He rose, walked to the window, and drawing the curtains looked out. The street was very quiet, but in the distance he thought he heard the tramp of a patrol. All the houses were dark and sullen; overhead the stars shone brightly; it was a perfect night to watch them.

He closed the window and taking a candle walked to a curtained door on one side of the room; it opened on a narrow, spiral stair which led to the flat roof. Most of the houses in Laurania were low, and Savrola when he reached the leads overlooked the sleeping city. Lines of gas-lamps marked the streets and squares, and brighter dots indicated the positions of the shipping in the harbour. But he did not long look at these; he was for the moment weary of men and their works. A small glass observatory stood in one corner of this aerial platform, the nose of the telescope showing through the aperture. He unlocked the door and entered. This was a side of his life that the world never saw; he was no mathematician intent on discovery or fame, but he loved to watch the stars for the sake of their mysteries. By a few manipulations the telescope was directed at the beautiful planet of Jupiter, at this time high in the northern sky. The glass was a powerful one, and the

14

great planet, surrounded by his attendant moons, glowed with splendour. The clock-work gear enabled him to keep it under continual observation as the earth rolled over with the hours. Long he watched it, becoming each moment more under the power of the spell that star-gazing exercises on curious, inquiring humanity.

At last he rose, his mind still far away from earth. Molara, Moret, the Party, the exciting scenes of the day, all seemed misty and unreal; another world, a world more beautiful, a world of boundless possibilities, enthralled his imagination. He thought of the future of Jupiter, of the incomprehensible periods of time that would elapse before the cooling process would render life possible on its surface, of the slow steady march of evolution, merciless, inexorable. How far would it carry them, the unborn inhabitants of an embryo world? Perhaps only to some vague distortion of the vital essence; perhaps further than he could dream of. All the problems would be solved, all the obstacles overcome; life would attain perfect developement. And then fancy, overleaping space and time, carried the story to periods still more remote. The cooling process would continue; the perfect developement of life would end in death; the whole solar system, the whole universe itself, would one day be cold and lifeless as a burned-out firework.

It was a mournful conclusion. He locked up the observatory and descended the stairs, hoping that his dreams would contradict his thoughts.

CHAPTER IV.

THE DEPUTATION.

It was the President's custom to rise early, but before doing so he invariably received the newspapers and read such remarks as dealt with the policy of the Government or criticised its actions. This morning his literature was exceptionally plentiful. All the papers had leading articles on the restriction of the franchise and the great riot which had followed its announcement. He first opened THE HOUR, the organ of orthodox mediocrity, which usually cautiously supported the Government in consideration of occasional pieces of news with which it was from time to time favoured. In a column and a half of print THE HOUR gently regretted that the President had been unable to restore the franchises unimpaired; it thus gratified the bulk of its readers. In a second column it expressed its severe disapproval—(unqualified condemnation was the actual term)—of the disgraceful riot which had led to such deplorable consequences; it thus repaid the President for sending round the text of the English note, which had arrived the night before, and which it printed verbatim with pomp and circumstance as coming from Our Special Correspondent in London.

THE COURTIER, the respectable morning journal of the upper classes, regretted that so unseemly a riot should have taken place at the beginning of the season, and expressed a hope that it would not in any way impair the brilliancy of the State Ball which was to take place on the 7th. It gave an excellent account of the President's first ministerial dinner, with the menu duly appended, and it was concerned to notice that Señor Louvet, Minister of the Interior, had been suffering from an indisposition which prevented his attending the function. THE DIURNAL GUSHER, a paper with an enormous circulation, refrained from actual comments but published an excellent account of the massacre, to the harrowing details of which it devoted much fruity sentiment and morbid imagination.

These were practically the organs on which the Government relied for support, and the President always read them first to fortify himself against the columns of abuse with which the Radical, Popular, and Democratic Press saluted him, his Government, and all his works. The worst result of an habitual use of strong language is that when a special occasion really does arise, there is no way of marking it. THE FABIAN, THE SUNSPOT, and THE RISING TIDE had already exhausted every epithet in their extensive vocabularies on other and less important incidents. Now that a severe fusilade had been made upon the citizens and an ancient privilege attacked, they were reduced to comparative moderation as the only outlet for their feelings. They had compared the Head of the State so often and so vividly to Nero and Iscariot, very much to the advantage of those worthies, that it was difficult to know how they could deal with him now. They nevertheless managed to find a few unused expressions, and made a great point of the Ministerial dinner as being an instance of his "brutal disregard of the commonest instincts of humanity." THE SUNSPOT was thought by its readers to have been particularly happy in alluding to the ministers as, "Indulging in a foul orgie of gluttony and dipping their blood-stained fingers in choice dishes, while the bodies of their victims lay unburied and unavenged."

Having finished his perusal the President pushed the last paper off the bed and frowned. He cared nothing for criticism, but he knew the power of the Press and he knew that it reflected as well as influenced public opinion. There could be no doubt that the balance was rising against him.

At breakfast he was moody and silent, and Lucile tactfully refrained from irritating him by the laboured commonplaces of matutinal conversation. By nine o'clock he was always at work and this morning he began earlier than usual. The Secretary was already at his table busily writing when Molara entered. He rose and bowed, a formal bow, which seemed an assertion of equality rather than a tribute of respect. The President nodded and walked to his table on which such parts of correspondence as needed his personal attention were neatly arranged. He sat down and began to read. Occasionally he uttered an exclamation of assent or disapproval, and his pencil was often employed to express his decisions and opinions. From time to time Miguel collected the papers he had thus dealt with and carried them to the inferior secretaries in the adjoining room, whose duty it was to elaborate into the stately pomposity of official language such phrases as "Curt Refusal" "Certainly not" "Apply to War Office" "Gushing Reply" "I do not agree" "See last year's Report."

Lucile also had letters to read and write. Having finished these she determined to take a drive in the park. For the last few weeks, since, in fact, they had returned from their summer residence, she had discontinued what had been in former years her usual practice; but after the scenes and riots of the day before she felt it her duty to display a courage which she did not feel. It might help her husband, for her beauty was such that an artistic

16

people invariably showed her respect. It could at least do no harm, and besides she was weary of the palace and its gardens. With this intention her carriage was ordered and she was about to enter it, when a young man arrived at the door. He saluted her gravely.

It was the boast of the citizens of the Republic of Laurania that they never brought politics into private life or private life into politics. How far they justified it will appear later. The present situation had undoubtedly strained the principle to the full, but civilities were still exchanged between political antagonists. Lucile, who had known the great Democrat as a frequent visitor at her father's house before the Civil War, and who had always kept up a formal acquaintance with him, smiled and bowed in return and asked whether he came to see the President.

"Yes," he replied. "I have an appointment."

"Public matters I suppose?" she inquired with the suspicion of a smile.

"Yes," he repeated somewhat abruptly.

"How tiresome you all are," she said daringly, "with your public businesses and solemn looks. I hear nothing but matters of State from morning till night, and now, when I fly the palace for an hour's relaxation, they meet me at the very door."

Savrola smiled. It was impossible to resist her charm. The admiration he had always felt for her beauty and her wit asserted itself in spite of the watchful and determined state of mind into which he had thrown himself as a preparation for his interview with the President. He was a young man, and Jupiter was not the only planet he admired. "Your Excellency," he said, "must acquit me of all intention."

"I do," she answered laughing, "and release you from all further punishment."

She signed to the coachman and bowing, drove off.

He entered the palace and was ushered by a footman resplendent in the blue and buff liveries of the Republic, into an ante-room. A young officer of the Guard, the Lieutenant who had commanded the escort on the previous day, received him. The President would be disengaged in a few minutes. The other members of the deputation had not yet arrived; in the meantime would he take a chair? The Lieutenant regarded him dubiously, as one might view some strange animal, harmless enough to look at, but about whose strength, when roused, there were extraordinary stories. He had been brought up in the most correct regimental ideas. the people (by which he meant the mob) were "swine"; their leaders were the same, with an adjective prefixed; democratic institutions, Parliament, and such like, were all "rot." It therefore appeared that he and Savrola would find few topics in common. But besides his good looks and good manners, the young soldier had other attainments; his men knew him as "all right" and "all there," while the Lancers of the Guard polo team regarded him as a most promising player.

Savrola, whose business it was to know everything, inquired respecting the project lately mooted by the Lauranian Cavalry of sending a polo team to England to compete in the great annual tournament at Hurlingham. Lieutenant Tiro (for that was his name) addressed himself to the subject with delight. They disputed as to who should be taken as "back." The discussion was only interrupted by the entrance of the Mayor and Renos, and the Subaltern went off to inform the President that the deputation waited.

"I will see them at once," said Molara; "show them up here."

The deputation were accordingly conducted up the stairs to the President's private room. He rose and received them with courtesy. Godoy stated the grievances of the citizens. He recalled the protests they had made against the unconstitutional government of the last five years, and their delight at the President's promise to call the Estates together. He described their bitter disappointment at the restriction of the franchise, and their keen desire that it should be fully restored. He dilated on their indignation at the cruelty with which the soldiers had shot down unarmed men, and finally declared that, as Mayor, he could not vouch for their continued loyalty to the President or their respect for his person. Renos spoke in the same strain, dwelling particularly on the legal aspect of the President's late action, and on the gravity of its effects as a precedent to posterity.

Molara replied at some length. He pointed out the disturbed state of the country, and particularly of the capital; he alluded to the disorders of the late war and the sufferings it had caused to the mass of the people. What the State wanted was strong stable government. As things became more settled the franchise should be extended until it would ultimately be completely restored. In the meanwhile, what was there to complain about? Law and order were maintained; the public service was well administered; the people enjoyed peace and security. More than that, a vigorous foreign policy held the honour of the country high. They should have an instance.

He turned and requested Miguel to read the reply to the English note on the African Dispute. The Secretary stood up and read the paper in question, his soft, purring voice, proving well suited to emphasising the insults it contained.

"And that, Gentlemen," said the President, when it was finished, "is addressed to one of the greatest military and naval powers in the world."

Godoy and Renos were silent. Their patriotism was roused; their pride was gratified; but Savrola smiled provokingly. "It will take more than despatches," he said, "to keep the English out of the African sphere, or to reconcile the people of Laurania to your rule."

"And if stronger measures should be necessary," said the President, "rest assured they will be taken."

"After the events of yesterday we need no such assurance."

The President ignored the taunt. "I know the English Government," he continued; "they will not appeal to arms."

"And I," said Savrola, "know the Lauranian people. I am not so confident."

There was a long pause. Both men faced each other, and their eyes met. It was the look of two swordsmen who engage, and it was the look of two bitter enemies; they appeared to measure distances and calculate chances. Then Savrola turned away, the ghost of a smile still lingering on his lips; but he had read the President's heart and he felt as if he had looked into hell.

"It is a matter of opinion, Sir," said Molara at last.

"It will soon be a matter of history."

"Other tales will have to be told before," said the President, and then with great formality, "I am obliged to you, Mr. Mayor and Gentlemen, for representing the dangerous elements of disorder which exist among certain classes of the people. You may rely on every precaution being taken to prevent an outbreak. I beg you will keep me further informed. Good morning."

The only course open appeared to be the door, and the deputation withdrew, after Savrola had thanked the President for his audience and had assured him that he would lose no opportunity of bringing home to him the hostile attitude of the citizens. On the way down-stairs they were met by Lucile, who had returned unexpectedly early from her drive. She saw by the expression of their faces that a heated discussion had taken place. Godoy and Renos she passed unnoticed, but she smiled merrily at Savrola, as if to convey to him that she was uninterested by politics and could not understand how people ever managed to get excited about them. The smile did not deceive him; he knew too much of her tastes and talents, but he admired her all the more for her acting.

He walked home. The interview had not been altogether unsatisfactory. He had never hoped to convince the President; that indeed was hardly likely; but they had expressed the views of the people, and Godoy and Renos had already sent copies of their remarks to the newspapers, so that the party could not complain of their leaders' inaction at such a crisis. He thought he had frightened Molara, if indeed it were possible to frighten such a man; at any rate he had made him angry. When he thought of this he was glad. Why? He had always hitherto repressed such unphilosophic and futile emotions so far as possible, but somehow to-day he felt his dislike of the President was invested with a darker tinge. And then his mind reverted to Lucile. What a beautiful woman she was! How full of that instinctive knowledge of human feelings which is the source of all true wit! Molara was a lucky man to have such a wife. Decidedly he hated him personally, but that, of course, was on account of his unconstitutional conduct.

When he reached his rooms, Moret was awaiting him, much excited and evidently angry. He had written several long letters to his leader, acquainting him with his unalterable decision to sever all connection with him and his party; but he had torn them all up, and was now resolved to tell him in plain words.

Savrola saw his look. "Ah, Louis," he cried, "I am glad you are here. How good of you to come! I have just left the President; he is recalcitrant; he will not budge an inch. I need your advice. What course shall we adopt?"

"What has happened?" asked the young man, sulkily but curiously.

19

Savrola related the interview with graphic terseness. Moret listened attentively and then said, still with great ill humour, "Physical force is the only argument he understands. I am for raising the people."

"Perhaps you are right," said Savrola reflectively, "I am half inclined to agree with you."

Moret argued his proposition with vigour and earnestness, and never had his leader seemed so agreeable to the violent measures he proposed. For half an hour they discussed the point. Savrola still appeared unconvinced; he looked at his watch. "It is past two o'clock," he said. "Let us lunch here and thrash the matter out."

They did so. The luncheon was excellent, and the host's arguments became more and more convincing. At last, with the coffee, Moret admitted that perhaps it was better to wait, and they parted with great cordiality.

CHAPTER V.

A PRIVATE CONVERSATION.

"That," said the President to his confidential secretary, so soon as the door had closed on the retiring deputation, "is over, but we shall have plenty more in the future. Savrola will most certainly be elected for the Central Division, and we shall then have the pleasure of listening to him in the Senate."

"Unless," added Miguel, "anything should happen."

The President, who knew his man well, understood the implication. "No, it is no good; we cannot do that. Fifty years ago it might have been possible. People won't stand that sort of thing now-a-days; even the army might have scruples. So long as he keeps within the law, I don't see how we can touch him constitutionally."

"He is a great force, a great force; sometimes, I think, the greatest in Laurania. Every day he grows stronger. Presently the end will come," said the Secretary slowly and thoughtfully, who, as the partner of Molara's dangers, no less than of his actions, had a claim to be heard. "I think the end is coming," he continued; "perhaps quite soon— unless——?" he paused.

"I tell you it can't be done. Any accident that happened would be attributed to me. It would mean a revolution here, and close every asylum abroad."

"There are other ways besides force, physical force."

"None that I can see, and he is a strong man."

"So was Samson, nevertheless the Philistines spoiled him."

"Through a woman. I don't believe he has ever been in love."

"That is no reason against the future."

"Wanted a Delilah," said the President dryly. "Perhaps you will find one for him."

The Secretary's eyes wandered round the room artlessly, and paused for a moment on a photograph of Lucile.

"How dare you, Sir! You are a scoundrel! You have not an ounce of virtue in you!"

"We have been associated for some time, General." He always called him General on these occasions, it reminded the President of various little incidents which had taken place when they had worked together during the war. "Perhaps that is the cause."

"You are impertinent."

"My interests are concerned. I too have enemies. You know very well how much my life would be worth without the protection of the Secret Police. I only remember with whom and for whom these things were done."

"Perhaps I am hasty, Miguel, but there is a limit, even between——" He was going to say friends but Miguel interposed accomplices. "Well," said Molara, "I do not care what you call it. What is your proposition?"

"The Philistines," replied Miguel, "spoiled Samson, but Delilah had to cut his hair first."

"Do you mean that she should implore him to hold his hand?"

"No, I think that would be useless, but if he were compromised——"

"But she, she would not consent. It would involve her."

"She need not necessarily know. Another object for making his acquaintance might be suggested. It would come as a surprise to her."

"You are a scoundrel—an infernal scoundrel," said the President quietly.

Miguel smiled, as one who receives a compliment. "The matter," he said, "is too serious for the ordinary rules of decency and honour. Special cases demand special remedies."

"She would never forgive me."

21

"The forgiveness would rest with you. Your charity would enable you to pardon an uncommitted crime. You have only to play the jealous husband and own your mistake later on."

"And he?"

"Fancy the great popular leader. Patriot, Democrat, what not, discovered fawning to the tyrant's wife! Why, the impropriety alone would disgust many. And more than that,— observe him begging for mercy, grovelling at the President's feet,—a pretty picture! It would ruin him; ridicule alone would kill him."

"It might," said Molara. The picture pleased him.

"It must. It is the only chance that I can see, and it need cost you nothing. Every woman is secretly flattered by the jealousy of the man she loves, even if he be her husband."

"How do you know these things?" asked Molara, looking at the ugly pinched figure and glistening hair of his companion.

"I know," said Miguel with a grin of odious pride. The suggestion of his appetites was repulsive. The President was conscious of disgust. "Mr. Secretary Miguel," he said with the air of one who has made up his mind, "I must request you not to speak to me of this matter again. I consider it shows less to the advantage of your heart than of your head."

"I see by Your Excellency's manner that further allusion is unnecessary."

"Have you the report of the Agricultural Committee for last year? Good,—please have a précis made of it; I want some facts. The country may be kept, even if we lose the capital; that means a good part of the army."

Thus the subject dropped. Each understood the other, and behind lay the spur of danger.

After the President had finished the morning's business, he rose to leave the room, but before he did so he turned to Miguel and said abruptly: "It would be a great convenience for us to know what course the Opposition intends to pursue on the opening of the Senate, would it not?"

"Assuredly."

"How can we induce Savrola to speak? He is incorruptible."

"There is another method."

"I tell you physical force is not to be thought of."

"There is another method."

"And that," said the President, "I directed you not to speak of again."

"Precisely," said the Secretary, and resumed his writing.

The garden into which Molara walked was one of the most beautiful and famous in a country where all vegetation attained luxuriant forms. The soil was fertile, the sun hot, and the rains plentiful. It displayed an attractive disorder. The Lauranians were no admirers of that peculiar taste which finds beauty in the exact arrangement of an equal number of small trees of symmetrical shape in mathematical designs, or in the creation of geometrical figures by means of narrow paths with box-hedges. They were an unenlightened people, and their gardens displayed a singular contempt for geometry and precision. Great blazes of colour arranged in pleasing contrasts were the lights, and cool green arbours the shades of their rural pictures. Their ideal of gardening was to make every plant grow as freely as if directed by nature, and to as high perfection as if cultivated by art. If the result was not artistic, it was at least beautiful.

The President, however, cared very little for flowers or their arrangement; he was, he said, too busy a man to have anything to do with the beauties of colour, harmony, or line. Neither the tints of the rose nor the smell of the jasmine awakened in him more than the rudimentary physical pleasures which are natural and involuntary. He liked to have a good flower garden, because it was the right thing to have, because it enabled him to take people there and talk to them personally on political matters, and because it was convenient for afternoon receptions. But he himself took no interest in it. The kitchen garden appealed to him more; his practical soul rejoiced more in an onion than an orchid.

He was full of thought after his conversation with Miguel, and turned down the shady path which led to the fountains with long, hasty strides. Things were looking desperate. It was, as Miguel had said, a question of time, unless,—unless Savrola were removed or discredited. He refrained from precisely formulating the idea that had taken possession of his mind. He had done many things in the rough days of the war when he was a struggling man, the memory of which was not pleasant. He remembered a brother officer, a rising man, the colonel of a regiment, who had been a formidable rival; at a critical moment he had withheld the supports, and left it to the enemy to remove one obstacle from his path. Then another tale came into his mind which also was not a pretty one, a tale of a destroyed treaty, and a broken truce; of men, who had surrendered to terms, shot against the wall of the fort they had held so long. He also recalled with annoyance the methods he had adopted to extract information from the captured spy; five years of busy life, of success and fortune, had not obscured the memory of the man's face as it writhed in suffering. But this new idea seemed the most odious of all. He was unscrupulous, but like many men in history or modern life, he had tried to put away a discreditable past. Henceforth, he had said when he obtained power, he would abandon such methods: they would no longer be necessary; and yet, here was the need already. Besides, Lucile was so beautiful; he loved her in his hard way for that alone; and she was such a consort, so tactful, so brilliant, that he admired and valued her from a purely official standpoint. If she ever knew, she would never forgive him. She never should know, but still he hated the idea.

23

But what other course remained? He thought of the faces of the crowd the day before; of Savrola; of the stories which reached him from the army; of other tales of a darker and more mysterious kind,—tales of strange federations and secret societies, which suggested murder, as well as revolution. The tide was rising; it was dangerous to tarry.

And then the alternative presented itself; flight, abdication, a squalid existence in some foreign country, despised, insulted, suspected; and exiles always lived to a great age he had heard. He would not think of it; he would die first; nothing but death should drag him from the palace, and he would fight to the last. His mind returned to the starting point of his reflections. Here was a chance, the one solution which seemed possible; it was not an agreeable one, but it was that or none. He had reached the end of the path and turning the corner saw Lucile seated by the fountain. It was a beautiful picture.

She saw his preoccupied look and rose to meet him. "What is the matter, Antonio? You look worried."

"Things are going wrong with us, my dear. Savrola, the deputation, the newspapers, and, above all, the reports I receive of the people, are ominous and alarming."

"I noticed black looks this morning when I drove. Do you think there is danger?"

"I do," he answered in his precise official manner, "grave danger."

"I wish I could help you," she said, "but I am only a woman. What can I do?" He did not answer and she continued: "Señor Savrola is a kind man. I used to know him quite well before the war."

"He will ruin us."

"Surely not."

"We shall have to fly the country, if indeed they allow us to do that."

She turned paler. "But I know what men look like; there is a sympathy between us; he is no fanatic."

"There are powers behind and beneath him of which he knows little, which he cannot control, but which he has invoked."

"Can you do nothing?"

"I cannot arrest him; he is too popular, and besides he has broken no law. He will go on. In a fortnight are the elections; he will be returned in spite of my precautions; then the trouble will begin." He paused, and then speaking as if to himself continued: "If we could learn what he means to do, perhaps we might defeat it."

"Can I not help you?" she asked quickly. "I know him; I think he likes me. He might whisper to me what he would not tell to others." She thought of many victories in the past.

24

"My darling," said Molara, "why should you spoil your life by mixing in the darker side of politics? I would not ask you."

"But I want to. I will try if it would help you."

"It might do much more."

"Very well, I will find out for you; in a fortnight you shall know. He must come to the State Ball; I will meet him there."

"I am loth to let you talk to such a man, but I know your wit, and the need is great. But will he come?"

"I will write him a note with the invitation," she said, "laugh at politics and advise him to keep his private life at least free from them. I think he will come; if not, I will find some other way of seeing him."

Molara looked at her with admiration. At no time did he love her more than when he realised of what use she was to him. "I leave it to you, then. I fear you will fail, but if you can do it, you may have saved the State. If not, no harm will have been done."

"I shall succeed," she answered confidently, and rising from her seat began to walk towards the house. She saw from her husband's manner that he would like to be alone.

He remained seated there for a long time, staring into the water in which the fat, lazy, gold fish swam placidly. His face wore the expression of one who has swallowed some nasty thing.


CHAPTER VI.

ON CONSTITUTIONAL GROUNDS.

The sagacious founders of the Lauranian Republic had recognised the importance of preserving and promoting the practice of social civilities between the public men of the State, irrespective of party. It had therefore long been the custom for the President to give several official entertainments during the autumn season, to which all the distinguished characters of either side were invited, and which it was considered etiquette to attend. This year feeling ran so high and relations were so strained that Savrola had decided not to accept, and had already formally declined the invitation; he was therefore not a little surprised when he received a second card, and still more when he read Lucile's note which accompanied it.

He saw she had exposed herself to a rebuff with her eyes open, and wondered why she had done so. Of course she counted on her charms. It is hard, if not impossible, to snub a beautiful woman; they remain beautiful and the rebuke recoils. He might indeed have made political capital out of so pressing an invitation sent at such a critical time; but he felt she had judged him well, and knew she was safe at least from that. This pleased him. He was sorry he could not go; but he had made up his mind, and sat down to write and decline. Half way through the letter, he paused; the thought occurred to him, that perhaps she might stand in need of his help. He read the letter again and fancied, though the words did not warrant it, that he detected a note of appeal. And then he began to look for reasons for changing his mind: the old established custom; the necessity of showing his followers that for the present he was in favour of constitutional agitation only; the opportunity of displaying his confidence in the success of his plans; in fact, every argument, but the true one, was arrayed against his determination.

Yes, he would go: the party might object, but he did not care; it was none of their business, and he was strong enough to face their displeasure. These reflections were interrupted by the entrance of Moret, his face glowing with enthusiasm.

"The Central Division Committee have nominated you unanimously as their candidate at the elections. The Dictator's puppet, Tranta, was howled down. I have arranged for a public meeting on Thursday night for you to address. We are on the crest of the wave!"

"Capital!" said Savrola. "I had expected to be nominated; our influence in the capital is supreme. I am glad of an opportunity of speaking; I have not had a meeting for some time, and there is a good deal to talk about just now. What day did you say you had arranged it for?"

"Thursday in the City-Hall at eight in the evening," said Moret, who, though sanguine, was not unbusiness-like.

"Thursday?"

"Yes, you are not engaged anywhere."

"Well," said Savrola speaking slowly and appearing to weigh his words, "Thursday is the night of the State Ball."

"I know," said Moret, "that was why I arranged it so. They will feel they are dancing on a volcano; only a mile from the palace will be the people, massed, agreed, determined. Molara will not enjoy his evening; Louvet will not go; Sorrento will be making arrangements to massacre, if necessary. It will spoil the festivities; they will all see the writing on the wall."

"Thursday will not do, Moret."

"Not do! Why not?"

"Because I am going to the ball that night," said Savrola deliberately.

26

Moret gasped. "What," he cried, "you!"

"Most certainly I shall go. The ancient customs of the State cannot be set aside like this. It is my duty to go; we are fighting for the Constitution, and we are bound to show our respect for its principles."

"You will accept Molara's hospitality,—enter his house,—eat his food?"

"No," said Savrola; "I shall eat the food provided by the State. As you well know, the expenses of these official functions are chargeable to the public."

"You will talk to him?"

"Certainly, but he will not enjoy it."

"You will insult him, then?"

"My dear Moret, what should make you think that? I shall be very civil. That will frighten him most of all; he will not know what is impending."

"You cannot go," said Moret decidedly.

"Indeed I am going."

"Think what the Trade-Unions will say."

"I have thought about all these things and have made up my mind," said Savrola. "They may say what they like. It will show them that I do not intend to discard Constitutional methods for a long time yet. These people want their enthusiasm cooling from time to time; they take life too seriously."

"They will accuse you of betraying the cause."

"I have no doubt stupid people will make characteristic remarks, but I trust none of my friends will bore me by repeating them to me."

"What will Strelitz say? It will very likely make him cross the frontier with his followers. He thinks we are lukewarm, and has been growing more impatient every week."

"If he comes before we are ready to help, the troops will make short work of him and his rabble. But he has definite orders from me and will, I hope, obey them."

"You are doing wrong, and you know it," said Moret harshly and savagely; "to say nothing of the contemptible humiliation of cringing to your enemy."

Savrola smiled at his follower's anger. "Oh," he said, "I shall not cringe. Come, you have not yet seen me do that," and he put his hand on his companion's arm. "It is strange, Louis," he continued, "that we differ in so many things, and yet, if I were in difficulty and

27

doubt, there is no one to whom I would go sooner than to you. We squabble about trifles, but if it were a great matter, your judgment should rule me, and you know it well."

Moret yielded. He always yielded to Savrola when he talked like that. "Well," he said, "when will you speak?"

"Whenever you like."

"Friday, then, the sooner the better."

"Very well; do you make the arrangements; I will find something to say."

"I wish you were not going," said Moret, reverting to his former objection; "nothing on earth would induce me to go."

"Moret," said Savrola with strange earnestness, "we have settled that; there are other things to talk about. I am troubled in my mind. There is an undercurrent of agitation, the force of which I cannot gauge. I am the acknowledged leader of the party, but sometimes I realise that there are agencies at work, which I do not control. That secret society they call the League is an unknown factor. I hate that fellow, that German fellow, Kreutze, Number One as he styles himself. He is the source of all the opposition I encounter in the party itself; the Labour Delegates all seem to be under his influence. Indeed there are moments when I think that you and I and Godoy and all who are striving for the old Constitution, are but the political waves of a social tide that is flowing we know not whither. Perhaps I am wrong, but I keep my eyes open and their evidence makes me thoughtful. The future is inscrutable but appalling; you must stand by me. When I can no longer restrain and control, I will no longer lead."

"The League is nothing," said Moret, "but a small anarchist group, who have thrown in their lot, for the present, with us. You are the indispensable leader of the party; you have created the agitation, and it is in your hands to stimulate or allay it. There are no unknown forces; you are the motive power."

Savrola walked to the window. "Look out over the city," he said. "It is a great mass of buildings; three hundred thousand people live there. Consider its size; think of the latent potentialities it contains, and then look at this small room. Do you think I am what I am, because I have changed all those minds, or because I best express their views? Am I their master or their slave? Believe me, I have no illusions, nor need you."

His manner impressed his follower. It almost seemed to him, as he watched the city and listened to Savrola's earnest words, that he heard the roar of a multitude, distant, subdued, but intense as the thunder of the surf upon a rocky coast when the wind is off the sea. He did not reply. His highly wrought temperament exaggerated every mood and passion; he always lived in the superlative. He had no counterpoise of healthy cynicism. Now he was very solemn, and bidding Savrola good-morning, walked slowly down the stairs, swayed by the vibrations of a powerful imagination which had been stimulated to an extreme.

28

Savrola lay back in his chair. His first inclination was to laugh, but he realised that his mirth would not be entirely at Moret's expense. He had tried to trick himself as well, but the parts of that subtle brain were too intimately connected to have secrets from one another. Still he would not allow them to formulate the true reason of his change of mind. It was not so, he said to himself several times, and even if it were it was of no importance and signified nothing. He took a cigarette from his case, and lighting it, watched the coiling rings of smoke.

How much of what he had said had he believed? He thought of Moret's serious face; that was not entirely produced by his influence. The young revolutionist had noticed something too, but had feared, or failed, to reduce his impressions to words. There was an undercurrent then; there were many dangers ahead. Well, he did not care; he was confident in his own powers. As the difficulties arose, he would meet them; when dangers threatened he would overcome them. Horse, foot, and artillery, he was a man, a complete entity. Under any circumstances, in any situation he knew himself a factor to be reckoned with; whatever the game, he would play it to his amusement, if not to his advantage.

The smoke of his cigarette curled round his head. Life,—how unreal, how barren, and yet, how fascinating! Fools, calling themselves philosophers, had tried to bring home the bitter fact to men. His philosophy lent itself to a pious fraud—taught him to minimise the importance of his pains, and to magnify that of his pleasures; made life delightful and death incidental. Zeno had shown him how to face adversity, and Epicurus how to enjoy pleasure. He basked in the smiles of fortune, and shrugged his shoulders at the frowns of fate. His existence, or series of existences, had been agreeable. All that he remembered had been worth living. If there was a future state, if the game was to begin again elsewhere, he would take a hand. He hoped for immortality, but he contemplated annihilation with composure. Meanwhile the business of living was an interesting problem. His speech,—he had made many and knew that nothing good can be obtained without effort. These impromptu feats of oratory existed only in the minds of the listeners; the flowers of rhetoric were hothouse plants.

What was there to say? Successive cigarettes had been mechanically consumed. Amid the smoke he saw a peroration, which would cut deep into the hearts of a crowd; a high thought, a fine simile, expressed in that correct diction which is comprehensible even to the most illiterate, and appeals to the most simple; something to lift their minds from the material cares of life and to awake sentiment. His ideas began to take the form of words, to group themselves into sentences; he murmured to himself; the rhythm of his own language swayed him; instinctively he alliterated. Ideas succeeded one another, as a stream flows swiftly by and the light changes on its waters. He seized a piece of paper and began hurriedly to pencil notes. That was a point; could not tautology accentuate it? He scribbled down a rough sentence, scratched it out, polished it, and wrote it in again. The sound would please their ears, the sense improve and stimulate their minds. What a game it was! His brain contained the cards he had to play, the world the stakes he played for.

As he worked, the hours passed away. The housekeeper entering with his luncheon found him silent and busy; she had seen him thus before and did not venture to interrupt him. The untasted food grew cold upon the table, as the hands of the clock moved slowly round marking the measured tread of time. Presently he rose, and, completely under the influence of his own thoughts and language, began to pace the room with short rapid strides, speaking to himself in a low voice and with great emphasis. Suddenly he stopped, and with a strange violence his hand descended on the table. It was the end of the speech.

The noise recalled him to the commonplaces of life. He was hungry and tired, and with a laugh at his own enthusiasm sat down at the table and began his neglected luncheon.

A dozen sheets of note paper, covered with phrases, facts, and figures, were the result of the morning's work. They lay pinned together on the table, harmless insignificant pieces of paper; and yet Antonio Molara, President of the Republic of Laurania, would have feared a bombshell less. Nor would he have been either a fool or a coward.

CHAPTER VII.

THE STATE BALL.

The palace of Laurania was admirably suited to the discharge of the social ceremonies of the State. The lavish expenditure on public entertainments, which the constitutional practice encouraged, allowed the hospitalities of the Republic to be extended upon the most magnificent scale. The opening State Ball of the season was in many ways the most important of these affairs. It was at this function that the great men of both parties met, for the first time after the summer heats, before the autumn session, and the brilliant society of the capital reunited after their absence in their country and mountain villas. Taste, elegance, and magnificence were equally displayed. The finest music, the best champagne, the most diverse, yet select, company were among the attractions of the evening. The spacious courtyard of the palace was completely covered by a gigantic awning. Rows of the Infantry of the Guard lined the approaches, and with their bright steel bayonets increased the splendour and the security of the occasion. The well-lit streets were crowded with the curious populace. The great hall of the palace, at all times imposing and magnificent, displayed a greater pomp when filled with a gaily dressed company.

At the head of the stairs stood the President and his wife, he resplendent in his orders and medals, she in her matchless beauty. As the guests ascended, an aide-de-camp, a gorgeous thing in crimson and gold, inquired their names and styles and announced them. Many and various was the company; every capital in Europe, every country in the world, was represented.

The guest of the evening was the King of Ethiopia, a mass of silk and jewels framing a black but vivacious face. He came early,—unwisely as, had he come later, there would have been a better audience to watch his arrival; however, to his untutored mind perhaps this was a matter of little importance.

The Diplomatic Corps followed in a long succession. Coach after coach drew up at the entrance and discharged its burden of polite astuteness, clothed in every conceivable combination of gold and colour. Arrived at the top of the stairs, the Russian Ambassador, grey but gallant, paused and, bowing with a stately courtesy, kissed the hand Lucile extended.

"The scene is an appropriate setting to a peerless diamond," he murmured.

"Would it sparkle as brightly in the Winter Palace?" inquired Lucile lightly.

"Assuredly the frosty nights of Russia would intensify its brilliancy."

"Among so many others it would be lost."

"Among all others it would be unrivalled and alone."

"Ah," she said, "I hate publicity, and as for solitude, frosty solitude, the thought of it alone makes me shiver."

She laughed. The diplomatist threw her a look of admiration, and stepping into the crowd, that already blocked the head of the stairs, received and returned the congratulations of his numerous friends.

"Madame Tranta," said the aide-de-camp.

"I am so glad to see you," said Lucile. "What a pity your daughter could not come; it has been a great disappointment to many."

The ugly old woman thus addressed beamed with delight, and moving up the stairs pushed her way to the marble balustrade of the balcony. She watched the later arrivals, and commented freely to her acquaintance on their dresses and deportments; she also gave a little information about each one, which would have been ill-natured even had it not been untrue; but though she told her friends many things, she did not mention that she had had to make Tranta write and threaten to desert the President's party unless she was asked to the ball, and that even this had failed to procure an invitation for her daughter, an unfortunate girl who added a bad complexion to the family features.

Louvet came next, looking anxiously at the crowd of faces which gazed from the landing, and imagining bombs and daggers at every step. He regarded Lucile with apprehension, but her smile seemed to give him courage and he mingled with the throng.

Then Sir Richard Shalgrove, the British Ambassador, whose genial and cheery face displayed an innocence which contrasted with his reputation, advanced to make his bow. The strained relations between Laurania and Great Britain seemed to disappear in that comprehensive salutation. Lucile engaged him for a moment in conversation; she pretended to know little or nothing. "And when," she asked merrily, "do we declare war?"

"Not until after I have had the pleasure of the third waltz, I hope," said the Ambassador.

31

"How annoying! I wanted so much to dance it with you."

"And you will not?" he asked in great concern.

"Dare I plunge two nations into war for the sake of a waltz?"

"Had you my inducement you would not hesitate," he replied gallantly.

"What, to precipitate hostilities! What have we done? What is your great inducement to fight?"

"Not to fight,—to dance," said Sir Richard with a little less than his usual assurance.

"For a diplomatist you are indeed explicit. While you are in so good a mood, tell me what has happened; is there danger?"

"Danger? No—how could there be?" He selected a formula: "Between traditionally friendly powers arbitration settles all disputes."

"You realise," she said earnestly and with an entire change of manner, "that we have to consider the political situation here? A strong despatch improves the position of the Government."

"I have felt all through," said the Ambassador uncompromisingly, "that there was no danger." He did not however mention that H.M. battleship Aggressor (12,000 tons displacement and 14,000 horse power, armed with four 11-inch guns) was steaming eighteen knots an hour towards the African port of the Lauranian Republic, or that he himself had been busy all the afternoon with cipher telegrams relating to ships, stores, and military movements. He thought that would be only boring her with purely technical details.

While this conversation had been taking place, the stream of people had passed continuously up the stairs, and the throng on the wide balcony that ran round the entire hall had become dense. The wonderful band was almost drowned by the hum of conversation; the perfect floor of the ball-room was only occupied by a few young couples whose own affairs absorbed their minds and excluded all other interests. A feeling of expectancy pervaded the hall; the rumour that Savrola would come had spread far and wide throughout Laurania.

Suddenly everyone became hushed, and above the strains of the band the distant sound of shouting was heard. Louder and louder it swelled, swiftly approaching until it was at the very gate; then it died away, and there was a silence through the hall filled only by the music. Had he been hooted or cheered? The sound had seemed strangely ambiguous; men were prepared to wager about it; his face would tell them the answer.

The swing-doors opened and Savrola entered. All eyes were turned on him, but his face showed them nothing, and the bets remained undecided. As he leisurely ascended the stairs, his eye travelled with interest round the crowded galleries and the brilliant throng who lined them. No decorations, no orders, no star relieved the plain evening dress he wore. Amid that blaze of colour, that multitude of gorgeous uniforms, he appeared a sombre figure; but, like the Iron Duke in Paris, he looked the leader of them all, calm, confident, and composed.

The President walked down a few steps to meet his distinguished guest. Both bowed with grave dignity.

"I am glad you have come, Sir," said Molara; "it is in harmony with the traditions of the State."

"Duty and inclination combined to point the way," answered Savrola with a smile marked by a suggestion of irony.

"You had no difficulty with the crowd?" suggested the President acidly.

"Oh, no difficulty, but they take politics a little seriously; they disapproved of my coming to your palace."

"You are right to come," said Molara. "Now we who are engaged in matters of State know what these things are worth; men of the world do not get excited over public affairs, nor do gentlemen fight with bludgeons."

"I prefer swords," said Savrola reflectively. He had reached the head of the stairs and Lucile stood before him. What a queen she looked, how peerless and incomparable among all women! The fine tiara she wore suggested sovereignty, and democrat as he was, he bowed to that alone. She held out her hand; he took it with reverence and courtesy, but the contact thrilled him.

The President selected a fat but famous woman from the aristocracy of Laurania, and led the way into the ball-room. Savrola did not dance; there were some amusements which his philosophy taught him to despise. Lucile was captured by the Russian Ambassador, and he remained a spectator.

Lieutenant Tiro saw him thus alone and approached him, wishing to finish their discussion about the "back" of the polo team, which had been interrupted the week before. Savrola received him with a smile; he liked the young soldier, as indeed did everyone. Tiro was full of arguments; he was in favour of a strong heavy player who should lie back in the game and take no chances. Savrola, having remarked on the importance of the Lauranian Army being properly represented in an international contest, favoured a light weight, playing right up to his forwards and ready to take the ball on himself at any moment. It was an animated discussion.

"Where have you played?" asked the Subaltern, surprised at his knowledge.

"I have never played the game," answered Savrola; "but I have always thought it a good training for military officers."

The subject was changed.

33

"Explain to me," said the great Democrat, "what all these different orders are. What is that blue one that Sir Richard, the British Ambassador, is wearing?"

"That is the Garter," replied the Subaltern; "the most honourable order in England."

"Really, and what is this that you are wearing?"

"I! Oh, that's the African medal. I was out there in '86 and '87, you know." As Savrola had anticipated, he was intensely pleased at being asked.

"It must have been a strange experience for you, who are so young."

"It was damned good fun," said the Subaltern with decision. "I was at Langi Tal. My squadron had a five-mile pursuit. The lance is a beautiful weapon. The English in India have a sport called pig-sticking; I have never tried it, but I know a better."

"Well, you may have another chance soon. We seem to be getting into difficulties with the British Government."

"Do you think there is any chance of war?" asked the boy eagerly.

"Well, of course," said Savrola, "a war would distract the attention of the people from internal agitation and the Reform movement. The President is a clever man. There might be war. I should not care to prophesy; but do you wish for it?"

"Certainly I do; it is my profession. I am sick of being a lap-dog in this palace; I long for the camp and the saddle again. Besides, these English will be worth fighting; they will give us a gallop all right. There was one of their officers with me at Langi Tal, a subaltern; he came as a spectator searching for adventure."

"What happened to him?"

"Well, you know, we pursued the enemy all the way to the hills and played the devil with them. As we were galloping along, he saw a lot making off towards a wood, and wanted to cut them off. I said there wasn't time; he laid me six to four there was, so I sent a troop,—I was in command of the squadron that day—you know. He went with them and showed them the way straight enough,—but I bore you?"

"On the contrary, I am greatly interested; what then?"

"He was wrong; the enemy got to the wood first and picked him off in the open. Our fellows brought him back, shot through the big artery of the leg; that doesn't take long, you know. All he said was: 'Well, you've won, but how the deuce you'll get paid, I can't think. Ask my brother,—Royal Lancers.'"

"And then?" asked Savrola.

34

"Well, I couldn't find the artery to compress it, and none of the doctors were about. He died,—a gallant fellow!"

The Subaltern paused, rather ashamed at having talked so much about his military adventures. Savrola felt as if he had looked into a new world, a world of ardent, reckless, warlike youth. He was himself young enough to feel a certain jealousy. This boy had seen what he had not; he possessed an experience which taught him lessons Savrola had never learned. Their lives had been different; but one day perhaps he would open this strange book of war, and by the vivid light of personal danger read the lessons it contained.

Meanwhile the dances had succeeded each other and the night was passing. The King of Ethiopia, horrified at the low dresses of the unveiled women and dreading the prospect of eating with odious white people, had taken his departure. The President, approaching Savrola, invited him to take his wife down to supper; a procession was formed; he offered Lucile his arm and they descended the stairs. The supper was excellent: the champagne was dry and the quails fat. A profusion of rare and beautiful orchids covered the table; Savrola's surroundings were agreeable, and he sat next the most beautiful woman in Laurania, who, though he did not know it, was exerting herself to captivate him. At first they talked amusing frivolities. The President, whose manners were refined, showed himself a pleasant companion and an accomplished talker. Savrola, who delighted in sparkling conversation, found it difficult to keep to the part of a purely official visitor which he had determined to observe. The influence of wit, wine, and beauty were combined to break his reserve; before he knew it, he had joined in a discussion, one of those half cynical, half serious discussions which are characteristic of an age which inquires because it doubts, and doubts the more because it has inquired.

The Russian Ambassador had said that he worshipped beauty, and had told his partner, the youthful Countess of Ferrol, that he regarded taking her into dinner as a religious observance.

"I suppose that means you are bored," she replied.

"By no means; in my religion the ceremonies are never dull; that is one of the principal advantages I claim for it."

"There are few others," said Molara; "you devote yourself to an idol of your own creation. If you worship beauty, your goddess stands on no surer pedestal than human caprice. Is it not so, Princess?"

The Princess of Tarentum, who was on the President's right, replied that even that foundation was more secure than that on which many beliefs repose.

"You mean that in your own case human caprice has been sufficiently constant? I can well believe it."

"No," she said; "I only mean that the love of beauty is common to all human beings."

35

"To all living things," corrected Savrola. "It is the love of the plant that produces the flower."

"Ah," said the President, "but, though the love of beauty may be constant, beauty itself may change. Look how everything changes: the beauty of one age is not the beauty of the next; what is admired in Africa is hideous in Europe. It is all a matter of opinion, local opinion. Your goddess, Monsieur, has as many shapes as Proteus."

"I like change," said the Ambassador. "I regard variability of form as a decided advantage in a goddess. I do not care how many shapes I look at, so long as all are beautiful."

"But," interposed Lucile, "you make no distinction between what is beautiful and what we think is beautiful."

"There is none," said the President.

"In Her Excellency's case there would be none," interposed the Ambassador politely.

"What is beauty," said Molara, "but what we choose to admire?"

"Do we choose? Have we the power?" asked Savrola.

"Certainly," answered the President; "and every year we alter our decisions; every year the fashion changes. Ask the ladies. Look at the fashions of thirty years ago; they were thought becoming then. Observe the different styles of painting that have succeeded each other, or of poetry, or of music. Besides, Monsieur de Stranoff's goddess, though beautiful to him, might not be so to another."

"I regard that also as a real advantage; you make me more enamoured with my religion each moment. I do not worship my ideals for the reclamé," said the Ambassador with a smile.

"You look at the question from a material point of view."

"Material rather than moral," said Lady Ferrol.

"But in the spirit-worship of my goddess the immorality is immaterial. Besides, if you say that our tastes are always changing, it seems to me that constancy is the essence of my religion."

"That is a paradox which we shall make you explain," said Molara.

"Well, you say I change each day, and my goddess changes too. To-day I admire one standard of beauty, to-morrow another, but when to-morrow comes I am no longer the same person. The molecular structure of my brain is altered; my ideas have changed; my old self has perished, loving its own ideal; the renovated ego starts life with a new one. It is all a case of wedded till death."

"You are not going to declare that constancy is a series of changes? You may as well assert that motion is a succession of halts."

"I am true to the fancy of the hour."

"You express my views in other words. Beauty depends on human caprice, and changes with the times."

"Look at that statue," said Savrola suddenly, indicating a magnificent marble figure of Diana which stood in the middle of the room surrounded by ferns. "More than two thousand years have passed since men called that beautiful. Do we deny it now?" There was no answer and he continued: "That is true beauty of line and form, which is eternal. The other things you have mentioned, fashions, styles, fancies, are but the unsuccessful efforts we make to attain to it. Men call such efforts art. Art is to beauty what honour is to honesty, an unnatural allotropic form. Art and honour belong to gentlemen; beauty and honesty are good enough for men."

There was a pause. It was impossible to mistake the democratic tone; his earnestness impressed them. Molara looked uneasy. The Ambassador came to the rescue.

"Well, I shall continue to worship the goddess of beauty, whether she be constant or variable"—he looked at the Countess; "and to show my devotion I shall offer up a waltz in that sacred fane, the ball-room."

He pushed his chair back, and, stooping, picked up his partner's glove, which had fallen to the floor. Everyone rose, and the party separated. As Savrola walked back to the hall with Lucile, they passed an open doorway leading to the garden. A multitude of fairy lights marked out the flower-beds or hung in festoons from the trees. The paths were carpeted with red cloth; a cool breeze fanned their faces. Lucile paused.

"It is a lovely night."

The invitation was plain. She had wanted to speak to him, then, after all. How right he was to come,—on constitutional grounds.

"Shall we go out?" he said.

She consented, and they stepped on to the terrace.

CHAPTER VIII.

"IN THE STARLIGHT."

The night was very still. The soft breeze was not strong enough to stir even the slender palms which rose on all sides, and whose outlines, above the surrounding foliage, framed the starlit sky. The palace stood on high ground, and the garden sloped on the western side towards the sea. At the end of the terrace was a stone seat.

"Let us sit here," said Lucile.

They sat down. The dreamy music of a waltz floated down as a distant accompaniment to their thoughts. The windows of the palace blazed with light and suggested glitter, glare, and heat; in the garden all was quiet and cool.

"Why do you sneer at honour?" asked Lucile, thinking of the interrupted conversation.

"Because it has no true foundation, no ultra-human sanction. Its codes are constantly changing with times and places. At one time it is thought more honourable to kill the man you have wronged than to make amends; at another it is more important to pay a bookmaker than a butcher. Like art it changes with human caprice, and like art it comes from opulence and luxury."

"But why do you claim a higher origin for beauty and honesty?"

"Because, wherever I have looked, I see that all things are perpetually referred to an eternal standard of fitness, and that right triumphs over wrong, truth over falsehood, beauty over ugliness. Fitness is the general expression! Judged by this standard art and honour have little value."

"But are these things so?" she asked wonderingly. "Surely there are many exceptions?"

"Nature never considers the individual; she only looks at the average fitness of the species. Consider the statistics of mortality. How exact they are: they give to a month the expectation of life to men; and yet they tell a man nothing. We cannot say that a good man will always overcome a knave; but the evolutionist will not hesitate to affirm that the nation with the highest ideals would succeed."

"Unless," said Lucile, "some other nation with lower ideals, but stronger arms, intervenes."

"Well, even then might is a form of fitness; I think a low form, but still physical force contains the elements of human progress. This is only the instance; we must enlarge our view. Nature does not consider the individual species. All we will now assert is that organisms imbued with moral fitness would ultimately rise above those whose virtue is physical. How many times has civilisation, by which I mean a state of society where moral force begins to escape from the tyranny of physical forces, climbed the ladder of Progress and been dragged down? Perhaps many hundred times in this world alone. But the motive power, the upward tendency, was constant. Evolution does not say 'always,' but 'ultimately.' Well, ultimately civilisation has climbed up beyond the reach of barbarism. The higher ideals have reached the surface by superior buoyancy."

38

"Why do you assume that this triumph is permanent? How do you know that it will not be reversed, as all others have been?"

"Because we have got might on our side, as well as moral ascendancy."

"Perhaps the Romans in the summit of their power thought that too?"

"Very likely, but without reason. They had only their swords to fall back upon as an ultimate appeal; and when they became effete they could no longer wield them."

"And modern civilisation?"

"Ah, we have other weapons. When we have degenerated, as we must eventually degenerate, when we have lost our intrinsic superiority, and other races, according to the natural law, advance to take our place, we shall fall back upon these weapons. Our morals will be gone, but our Maxims will remain. The effete and trembling European will sweep from the earth by scientific machinery the valiant savages who assail him."

"Is that the triumph of moral superiority?"

"At first it would be, for the virtues of civilisation are of a higher type than those of barbarism. Kindness is better than courage, and charity more than strength. But ultimately the dominant race will degenerate, and as there will be none to take its place, the degeneration must continue. It is the old struggle between vitality and decay, between energy and indolence; a struggle that always ends in silence. After all, we could not expect human developement to be constant. It is only a question of time before the planet becomes unfitted to support life on its surface."

"But you said that fitness must ultimately triumph."

"Over relative unfitness, yes. But decay will involve all, victors and vanquished. The fire of life will die out, the spirit of vitality become extinct."

"In this world perhaps."

"In every world. All the universe is cooling—dying, that is,—and as it cools, life for a spell becomes possible on the surface of its spheres, and plays strange antics. And then the end comes; the universe dies and is sepulchred in the cold darkness of ultimate negation."

"To what purpose then are all our efforts?"

"God knows," said Savrola cynically; "but I can imagine that the drama would not be an uninteresting one to watch."

"And yet you believe in an ultra-human foundation, an eternal ideal for such things as beauty and virtue."

"I believe that the superiority of fitness over relative unfitness is one of the great laws of matter. I include all kinds of fitness,—moral, physical, mathematical."

"Mathematical!"

"Certainly; words only exist by conforming to correct mathematical principles. That is one of the great proofs we have that mathematics have been discovered, not invented. The planets observe a regular progression in their distances from the sun. Evolution suggests that those that did not observe such principles were destroyed by collisions and amalgamated with others. It is a universal survival of the fittest." She was silent. He continued: "Now let us say that in the beginning there existed two factors, matter animated by the will to live, and the eternal ideal; the great author and the great critic. It is to the interplay and counter-action of these two that all developement, that all forms of life are due. The more the expression of the will to live approximates to the eternal standard of fitness, the better it succeeds."

"I would add a third," she said; "a great Being to instil into all forms of life the desire to attain to the ideal; to teach them in what ways they may succeed."

"It is pleasant," he replied, "to think that such a Being exists to approve our victories, to cheer our struggles, and to light our way; but it is not scientifically or logically necessary to assume one after the two factors I have spoken of are once at work."

"Surely the knowledge that such an ultra-human ideal existed must have been given from without."

"No; that instinct which we call conscience was derived as all other knowledge from experience."

"How could it be?"

"I think of it in this way. When the human race was emerging from the darkness of its origin and half animal, half human creatures trod the earth, there was no idea of justice, honesty, or virtue, only the motive power which we may call the 'will to live.' Then perhaps it was a minor peculiarity of some of these early ancestors of man to combine in twos and threes for their mutual protection. The first alliance was made; the combinations prospered where the isolated individuals failed. The faculty of combination appeared to be an element of fitness. By natural selection only the combinations survived. Thus man became a social animal. Gradually the little societies became larger ones. From families to tribes, and from tribes to nations the species advanced, always finding that the better they combined, the better they succeeded. Now on what did this system of alliance depend? It depended on the members keeping faith with each other, on the practice of honesty, justice, and the rest of the virtues. Only those beings in whom such faculties were present were able to combine, and thus only the relatively honest men were preserved. The process repeated itself countless times during untold ages. At every step the race advanced, and at every step the realisation of the cause increased. Honesty and justice are bound up in our compositions and form an inseparable part of our natures. It is only with difficulty that we repress such awkward inclinations."

40

"You do not then believe in God?"

"I never said that," said Savrola. "I am only discussing the question of our existence from one standpoint, that of reason. There are many who think that reason and faith, science and religion, must be everlastingly separated, and that if one be admitted the other must be denied. Perhaps it is because we see so short a span, that we think that their lines are parallel and never touch each other. I always cherish the hope that somewhere in the perspective of the future there may be a vanishing point where all lines of human aspiration will ultimately meet."

"And you believe all this that you have said?"

"No," he answered, "there is no faith in disbelief, whatever the poets have said. Before we can solve the problems of existence we must establish the fact that we exist at all. It is a strange riddle, is it not?"

"We shall learn the answer when we die."

"If I thought that," said Savrola, "I should kill myself to-night out of irresistible curiosity."

He paused, and looked up at the stars, which shone so brightly overhead. She followed his gaze. "You like the stars?" she asked.

"I love them," he replied; "they are very beautiful."

"Perhaps your fate is written there."

"I have always admired the audacity of man in thinking that a Supreme Power should placard the skies with the details of his squalid future, and that his marriage, his misfortunes, and his crimes should be written in letters of suns on the background of limitless space. We are consequential atoms."

"You think we are of no importance?"

"Life is very cheap. Nature has no exaggerated idea of its value. I realise my own insignificance, but I am a philosophic microbe, and it rather adds to my amusement than otherwise. Insignificant or not, I like living, it is good to think of the future."

"Ah," said Lucile impetuously, "whither are you hurrying us in the future,—to revolution?"

"Perhaps," said Savrola calmly.

"You are prepared to plunge the country in a civil war?"

"Well, I hope it will not come to that extreme. Probably there will be some street-fighting and some people will be killed, but——"

41

"But why should you drive them like this?"

"I discharge a duty to the human species in breaking down a military despotism. I do not like to see a Government supported only by bayonets; it is an anachronism."

"The Government is just and firm; it maintains law and order. Why should you assail it merely because it does not harmonise with your theories?"

"My theories!" said Savrola. "Is that the name you give to the lines of soldiers with loaded rifles that guard this palace, or to the Lancers I saw spearing the people in the square a week ago?"

His voice had grown strangely vehement and his manner thrilled her. "You will ruin us," she said weakly.

"No," he replied with his grand air, "you can never be ruined. Your brilliancy and beauty will always make you the luckiest of women, and your husband the luckiest of men."

His great soul was above the suspicion of presumption. She looked up at him, smiled quickly, and impulsively held out her hand. "We are on opposite sides, but we will fight under the rules of war. I hope we shall remain friends even though——"

"We are officially enemies," said Savrola, completing the sentence, and taking her hand in his he bowed and kissed it. After that they were both very silent, and walking along the terrace re-entered the palace. Most of the guests had already gone, and Savrola did not ascend the stairs, but passing through the swing-doors took his departure. Lucile walked up to the ball-room in which a few youthful and indefatigable couples were still circling. Molara met her. "My dear," he said, "where have you been all this time?"

"In the garden," she replied.

"With Savrola?"

"Yes."

The President repressed a feeling of satisfaction. "Did he tell you anything?" he asked.

"Nothing," she answered, remembering for the first time the object with which she had sought the interview; "I must see him again."

"You will continue to try and find out his political intentions?" inquired Molara anxiously.

"I shall see him again," she replied.

"I trust to your wit," said the President; "you can do it, if anyone can, my dearest."

The last dance came to an end and the last guest departed. Very weary and thoughtful Lucile retired to her room. Her conversation with Savrola filled her mind; his earnestness, his enthusiasm, his hopes, his beliefs, or, rather, his disbeliefs, all passed again in review before her. What a great man he was! Was it wonderful the people followed him? She would like to hear him speak to-morrow.

Her maid came in to assist her to undress. She had looked from an upper balcony and had seen Savrola. "Was that," she asked her mistress curiously, "the great Agitator?" Her brother was going to hear him make his speech to-morrow.

"Is he going to make a speech to-morrow?" asked Lucile.

"So my brother says," said the maid; "he says that he is going to give them such a dressing down they will never forget it." The maid paid great attention to her brother's words. There was much sympathy between them; in fact she only called him her brother because it sounded better.

Lucile took up the evening paper which lay on the bed. There on the first page was the announcement, the great meeting would take place at the City-Hall at eight the next evening. She dismissed the maid and walked to the window. The silent city lay before her; to-morrow the man she had talked with would convulse that city with excitement. She would go and hear him; women went to these meetings; why should she not go, closely veiled? After all it would enable her to learn something of his character and she could thus better assist her husband. With this reflection, which was extremely comforting, she went to bed.

The President was going up-stairs, when Miguel met him. "More business?" he asked wearily.

"No," said the Secretary; "things are going on very well."

Molara looked at him with quick annoyance; but Miguel's face remained impassive, so he simply replied, "I am glad of that," and passed on.

CHAPTER IX.

THE ADMIRAL.

The disapproval which Moret had expressed at Savrola's determination to go to the State Ball was amply justified by the result. Every paper, except those actually controlled by the party organisation, commented severely or contemptuously on his action. THE HOUR alluded to the groans with which the crowd had received him, as marking the decline of his influence with the masses and the break-up of the Revolutionary party. It also reminded its readers that social distinction was always the highest ambition of the

43

Demagogue, and declared that, by accepting the President's invitation, Savrola had revealed "his sordid personal aims." The other Government organs expressed a similar opinion in an even more offensive manner. "These agitators," said THE COURTIER, "have at all times in the history of the world hankered after titles and honours, and the prospect of mixing with persons of rank and fashion has once again proved irresistible to an austere and unbending son of the people." This superior vulgarity, though more unpleasant, was less dangerous than the grave and serious warnings and protests which the Democratic journals contained. THE RISING TIDE said plainly that, if this sort of thing continued, the Popular party would have to find another leader, "One who did not cringe to power nor seek to ingratiate himself with fashion."

Savrola read these criticisms with disdain. He had recognised the fact that such things would be said, and had deliberately exposed himself to them. He knew he had been unwise to go: he had known that from the first; and yet somehow he did not regret his mistake. After all, why should his party dictate to him how he should rule his private life? He would never resign his right to go where he pleased. In this case he had followed his own inclination, and the odium which had been cast upon him was the price he was prepared to pay. When he thought of his conversation in the garden, he did not feel that he had made a bad bargain. The damage however must be repaired. He looked over the notes of his speech again, polished his sentences, considered his points, collected his arguments, and made some additions which he thought appropriate to the altered state of public feeling.

In this occupation the morning passed. Moret came in to luncheon. He refrained from actually saying "I told you so," but his looks showed that he felt his judgment was for the future established on unshakable foundations. His was a character easily elated or depressed. Now he was gloomy and despondent, regarding the cause as already lost. Only a forlorn hope remained; Savrola might express his regret at the meeting, and appeal to the people to remember his former services. He suggested this to his leader, who laughed merrily at the idea. "My dear Louis," he said, "I shall do nothing of the sort. I will never resign my own independence; I shall always go where I like and do what I like, and if they are not pleased, they can find someone else to discharge their public business." Moret shuddered. Savrola continued: "I shall not actually tell them so, but my manner will show them that I fear their reproaches as little as Molara's enmity."

"Perhaps they will not listen; I hear reports that there will be some hostility."

"Oh, I shall make them listen. There may be some howling at first, but they will change their note before I have gone very far."

His confidence was contagious. Moret's spirits revived under its influence and that of a bottle of excellent claret. Like Napoleon the Third, he felt that all might yet be regained.

Meanwhile the President was extremely well satisfied with the first result of his schemes. He had not foreseen that Savrola's acceptance of the invitation to the ball would involve him in so much unpopularity, and, although it was a poor compliment to himself, it was an unexpected advantage. Besides, as Miguel had remarked, everything was going on very well in other directions. He had hardened his heart and dismissed his scruples;

44

stern, bitter necessity had thrust him on an unpleasant course, but now that he had started he was determined to go on. In the meantime affairs pressed on all sides. The British Government were displaying an attitude of resolution on the African Question. His violent despatch had not settled the matter, as he had hoped and even anticipated; it had become necessary to supplement his words by actions. The African port must not be left undefended; the fleet must go there at once. It was not a moment when he could well afford to be without the five ships of war whose presence in the harbour overawed many of the discontented; but he felt that a vigorous foreign policy would be popular, or at least sufficiently interesting to keep the public mind from domestic agitation. He also knew that a disaster abroad would precipitate a revolution at home. It was necessary to be very careful. He recognised the power and resources of Great Britain; he had no illusions on the subject of the comparative weakness of Laurania. In that indeed lay their only strength. The British Government would do all in their power to avoid fighting (bullying, polite Europe would call it) so small a State. It was a game of bluff; the further he could go, the better for the situation at home, but one step too far meant ruin. It was a delicate game to play, and it taxed to the utmost the energies and talents of a strong, able man.

"The Admiral is here, Your Excellency," said Miguel entering the room, followed immediately by a short, red-faced man in naval uniform.

"Good-morning, my dear de Mello," cried the President, rising and shaking the newcomer's hand with great cordiality. "I have got some sailing-orders for you at last."

"Well," said de Mello bluntly, "I am sick of lying up waiting for your agitators to rise."

"There is work of a difficult and exciting nature before you. Where's that translation of the cipher telegram, Miguel? Ah, thank you,—look here, Admiral."

The sailor read the paper, and whistled significantly. "It may go further than you wish, Molara, this time," he said unceremoniously.

"I shall place the matter in your hands; you will be able to save this situation, as you have saved so many others."

"Where did this come from?" asked de Mello.

"From French sources."

"She is a powerful ship, the Aggressor,—latest design, newest guns, in fact all the modern improvements; I have nothing that she could not sink in ten minutes; besides, there are some gunboats there as well."

"I know the situation is difficult," said the President; "that is why I am entrusting it to you! Now listen; whatever happens I don't want fighting; that would only end in disaster; and you know what disaster would mean here. You must argue and parley and protest on every point, and cause as much delay as possible. Consult me by telegraph on every occasion, and try to make friends with the English admiral; that is half the battle. If it ever comes to a question of bombardment, we shall give in and protest again. I will

45

have your instructions forwarded to you in writing this evening. You had better steam to-night. You understand the game?"

"Yes," said de Mello, "I have played it before." He shook hands and walked to the door.

The President accompanied him. "It is possible," he said earnestly, "that I shall want you back here before you have gone very far; there are many signs of trouble in the city, and after all Strelitz is still on the frontier waiting for a chance. If I send for you, you will come?" There was almost an appealing note in his tone.

"Come?" said the Admiral. "Of course I will come,—full steam ahead. I have had my big gun trained on the Parliament House for the last month, and I mean to let it off one day. Oh, you can trust the fleet."

"Thank God I never doubted that," said the President with some emotion, and shaking de Mello's hand warmly, he returned to his writing-table. He felt that the Admiral was thoroughly loyal to the Government.

These men who live their lives in great machines, become involved in the mechanism themselves. De Mello had lived on warships all his days, and neither knew nor cared for anything else. Landsmen and civilians he despised with a supreme professional contempt. Such parts of the world as bordered on the sea, he regarded as possible targets of different types; for the rest he cared nothing. With equal interest he would burst his shells on patriots struggling to be free or foreign enemies, on a hostile fort or on his native town. As long as the authority to fire reached him through the proper channel, he was content; after that he regarded the question from a purely technical standpoint.

The afternoon was far advanced before the President finished the varied labours of his office. "There is a great meeting to-night, is there not?" he asked Miguel.

"Yes," said the Secretary, "in the City-Hall; Savrola is going to speak."

"Have you arranged about an opposition?"

"Some of the secret police are going to make a little, I believe; Colonel Sorrento has arranged that. But I fancy Señor Savrola's party are rather displeased with him, as it is."

"Ah," said Molara, "I know his powers; he will tear their very hearts out with his words. He is a terrible force; we must take every precaution. I suppose the troops have been ordered to be under arms? There is nothing he cannot do with a crowd,—curse him!"

"The Colonel was here this morning; he told me he was making arrangements."

"It is good," said the President; "he knows his own safety is involved. Where do I dine to-night?"

"With Señor Louvet, at the Home Office, an official dinner."

46

"How detestable! Still he has a plain cook and he will be worth watching to-night. He gets in such a state of terror when Savrola holds forth that he is ridiculous. I hate cowards, but they make the world the merrier."

He bade the Secretary good-night and left the room. Outside he met Lucile. "Dearest," he said, "I am dining out to-night, an official dinner at Louvet's. It is a nuisance, but I must go. Perhaps I shall not be back till late. I am sorry to leave you like this, but in these busy days I can hardly call my soul my own."

"Never mind, Antonio," she replied; "I know how you are pressed with work. What has happened about the English affair?"

"I don't like the situation at all," said Molara. "They have a Jingo Government in power and have sent ships as an answer to our note. It is most unfortunate. Now I have to send the fleet away,—at such a moment." He groaned moodily.

"I told Sir Richard that we had to think of the situation here, and that the despatch was meant for domestic purposes," said Lucile.

"I think," said the President, "that the English Government also have to keep the electorate amused. It is a Conservative ministry; they must keep things going abroad to divert the public mind from advanced legislation. What, more still, Miguel?"

"Yes, Sir; this bag has just arrived, with several important despatches which require your immediate attention."

The President looked for a moment as if he would like to tell Miguel to take himself and his despatches to the infernal regions; but he repressed the inclination. "Good, I will come. I shall see you at breakfast to-morrow, my dear, till then, farewell," and giving her a weary smile he walked off.

Thus it is that great men enjoy the power they risk their lives to gain and often meet their deaths to hold.

Lucile was left alone, not for the first time when she had wanted companionship and sympathy. She was conscious of an unsatisfactory sensation with regard to existence generally. It was one of those moments when the prizes and penalties of life seem equally stale and futile. She sought refuge in excitement. The project she had conceived the night before began to take actual shape in her mind; yes, she would hear him speak. Going to her room she rang the bell. The maid came quickly. "What time is the meeting to-night?"

"At eight, Your Excellency," said the girl.

"You have a ticket for it?"

"Yes, my brother——"

"Well, give it to me; I want to hear this man speak. He will attack the Government; I must be there to report to the President."

The maid looked astonished, but gave up the ticket meekly. For six years she had been Lucile's maid, and was devoted to her young and beautiful mistress. "What will Your Excellency wear?" was her only remark.

"Something dark, with a thick veil," said Lucile. "Don't speak of this to anyone."

"Oh no, Your Ex——"

"Not even to your brother."

"Oh, no, Your Excellency."

"Say I have a headache and have gone to bed. You must go to your room yourself."

The maid hurried off to get the dress and bonnet. Lucile felt full of the nervous excitement her resolve had raised. It was an adventure, it would be an experience, more than that, she would see him. The crowd,—when she thought of them she felt a little frightened, but then she remembered that women frequently went to these demonstrations, and there would be plenty of police to keep order. She dressed herself hastily in the clothes that the maid brought, and descending the stairs, entered the garden. It was already dusk, but Lucile had no difficulty in finding her way to a small private gate in the wall, which her key unlocked.

She stepped into the street. All was very quiet. The gas lamps flared in a long double row till they almost met in the distant perspective. A few people were hurrying in the direction of the City-Hall. She followed them.

CHAPTER X.

THE WAND OF THE MAGICIAN.

The City-Hall was a gigantic meeting-house in which for many years all the public discussions of the Lauranian people had taken place. Its stone façade was showy and pretentious, but the building itself consisted merely of the great hall and of a few smaller rooms and offices. The hall was capable of holding nearly seven thousand people; with its white-washed roof sustained by iron girders, and well lit with gas, it served its purpose well without any affectation of display.

Lucile was caught in the stream of those who were entering and carried inside. She had expected to find a seat, but, in view of a great crowd, all the chairs had been removed from the body of the hall, and only standing room remained. In this solid mass of humanity she found herself an atom. To move was difficult; to go back almost impossible.

It was a striking scene. The hall, which was hung with flags, was crowded to overflowing; a long gallery, which ran round three sides, was densely packed to the very ceiling; the flaring gas-jets threw their yellow light on thousands of faces. The large majority of the audience were men, but Lucile noticed with relief that there were several women present. A platform at the far end of the hall displayed the customary table and the inevitable glass of water. In front of the platform were two long rows of reporters, getting their pads and pencils ready,—a kind of orchestra. Behind and above were again rows and rows of chairs filled by the numerous delegates, officials, and secretaries of the various political clubs and organisations, each distinguished by the badge and sash of his society. Moret had exerted himself to whip up the utmost power of the Party, and had certainly succeeded in organising the greatest demonstration Laurania had ever seen. All the political forces arrayed against the Government were represented.

There was a loud hum of conversation, broken at intervals by cheers and the choruses of patriotic songs. Suddenly the clock in the tower of the building chimed the hour. At the same instant, from a doorway on the right of the platform, Savrola entered, followed by Godoy, Moret, Renos, and several other prominent leaders of the movement. He made his way along the row of chairs, until he reached that on the right of the table, sat down and looked quietly about him. There was a storm of discordant shouting, no two men seeming to hold the same opinion. At one moment it sounded as if all were cheering; at another hoots and groans obtained the supremacy. The meeting in fact was about equally divided. The extreme sections of the Reform' Party, regarding Savrola's attendance at the ball as an action of the grossest treachery, howled with fury at him; the more moderate cheered him as the safest man to cling to in times of civil disturbance. The delegates and regular officials, who occupied the chairs on the platform, were silent and sullen, like men who await an explanation without belief in its sufficiency.

At length the shouting ceased. Godoy, who was in the chair, rose and made a short speech, in which he studiously avoided any contentious allusion to Savrola, confining himself only to the progress of the movement. He spoke well and clearly, but nobody wanted to hear him, and all were relieved when he concluded by calling upon "our leader," Savrola, to address the meeting. Savrola, who had been talking unconcernedly with one of the delegates on his right, turned round quickly towards the audience, and rose. As he did so, a man in a blue suit, one of a little group similarly clad, shouted out, "Traitor and toady!" Hundreds of voices took up the cry; there was an outburst of hooting and groaning; others cheered half-heartedly. It was an unpromising reception. Moret looked around him in blank despair.

In spite of the heat and the pressure, Lucile could not take her eyes off Savrola. She could see that he was quivering with suppressed excitement. His composure had merely been assumed; crowds stirred his blood, and when he rose he could wear his mask no longer. He looked almost terrible, as he waited there, facing the outburst with defiance written in every line of his pale, earnest face and resolute figure. Then he began to speak, but his words could not at first be distinguished through the persistent shouts of the man in blue and his friends. At length, after five minutes of intense disorder, the curiosity of the audience triumphed over all other emotions, and they generally sank into silence, to hear what their leader had to say.

Again Savrola began. Though he spoke very quietly and slowly, his words reached the furthest ends of the hall. He showed, or perhaps he feigned, some nervousness at first, and here and there in his sentences he paused as if searching for a word. He was surprised, he said, at his reception. He had not expected, now when the final result was so nearly attained, that the people of Laurania would change their minds. The man in blue began to howl his odious cry. There was another outbreak of hooting; but the majority of the audience were now anxious to listen, and silence was soon restored. Savrola continued. He briefly reviewed the events of the last year: the struggle they had had to form a party at all; the fierce opposition they had encountered and sustained; the success that had attended their threat of taking arms; the President's promise of a free Parliament; the trick that had been played on them; the firing of the soldiery on the crowd. His earnest, thoughtful words evoked a hum of approval. These were events in which the audience had participated, and they liked having them recalled to their memories.

Then he went on to speak of the Deputation and of the contempt with which the President had thought fit to treat the accredited representatives of the citizens. "Traitor and toady!" shouted the man in blue loudly; but there was no response. "And," said Savrola, "I will invite your attention to this further matter. It has not been sufficient to strangle the Press, to shoot down the people, and to subvert the Constitution, but even when we are assembled here in accordance with our unquestioned right to discuss matters of State and decide upon our public policies, our deliberations are to be interrupted by the paid agents of the Government,"—he looked towards the man in blue, and there was an angry hum—"who insult by their abusive cries not only myself, a free Lauranian, but you also, the assembled citizens who have invited me to place my views before you." Here the audience broke out into indignant applause and agreement; cries of "Shame!" were heard, and fierce looks turned in the direction of the interrupters, who had, however, dispersed themselves unobtrusively among the crowd. "In spite of such tactics," Savrola continued, "and in the face of all opposition, whether by bribes or bullets, whether by hired bravos or a merciless and mercenary soldiery, the great cause we are here to support has gone on, is going on, and is going to go on, until at length our ancient liberties are regained, and those who have robbed us of them punished." Loud cheers rose from all parts of the hall. His voice was even and not loud, but his words conveyed an impression of dauntless resolution.

And then, having got his audience in hand, he turned his powers of ridicule upon the President and his colleagues. Every point he made was received with cheers and laughter. He spoke of Louvet, of his courage, and of his trust in the people. Perhaps, he said, it was not inappropriate that the Ministry of the Interior should be filled by "a glutton," the Home Office by a "stay-at-home" who was afraid to go out among his countrymen at night. Louvet was indeed a good object for abuse; he was hated by the people, who despised his cowardice and had always jeered at him. Savrola continued. He described the President as clinging to office at whatever cost to himself or others. In order to draw the attention of the people from his tyrannical actions and despotic government at home, he had tried to involve them in complications abroad, and he had succeeded, more completely than he had bargained for. They were embroiled now in a dispute with a great Power, a dispute from which they had nothing to gain and everything to lose. Their fleets and armies must be despatched, to the cost of the State; their possessions were endangered; perhaps the lives of their soldiers and sailors would be sacrificed. And all for what? In order that Antonio Molara might do as he had declared he would, and die at the head of the State. It was a bad joke. But he should be warned; many a true word was spoken in jest. Again there was a fierce hum.

Lucile listened spell-bound. When he had risen, amid the groans and hisses of that great crowd, she had sympathised with him, had feared even for his life, had wondered at the strange courage which made him attempt the seemingly impossible task of convincing such an audience. As he had progressed and had begun to gain power and approval, she had rejoiced; every cheer had given her pleasure. She had silently joined in the indignation which the crowd had expressed against Sorrento's police-agents. Now he was attacking her husband; and yet she hardly seemed to feel an emotion of antagonism.

He left the subject of the Ministers with contemptuous scorn, amid the earnest assent of the audience and on the full tide of public opinion. They must now, he said, treat of higher matters. He invited them to consider the ideals at which they aimed. Having roused their tempers, he withheld from them the outburst of fury and enthusiasm they desired. As he spoke of the hopes of happiness to which even the most miserable of human beings had a right, silence reigned throughout the hall, broken only by that grave melodious voice which appealed to everyone. For more than three quarters of an hour he discussed social and financial reforms. Sound practical common sense was expressed with many a happy instance, many a witty analogy, many a lofty and luminous thought.

"When I look at this beautiful country that is ours and was our fathers before us, at its blue seas and snow-capped mountains, at its comfortable hamlets and wealthy cities, at its silver streams and golden corn-fields, I marvel at the irony of fate which has struck across so fair a prospect the dark shadow of a military despotism."

The sound of momentous resolution rose again from the crowded hall. He had held their enthusiasm back for an hour by the clock. The steam had been rising all this time. All were searching in their minds for something to relieve their feelings, to give expression to the individual determination each man had made. There was only one mind throughout the hall. His passions, his emotions, his very soul appeared to be communicated to the seven thousand people who heard his words; and they mutually inspired each other.

Then at last he let them go. For the first time he raised his voice, and in a resonant, powerful, penetrating tone which thrilled the listeners, began the peroration of his speech. The effect of his change of manner was electrical. Each short sentence was followed by wild cheering. The excitement of the audience became indescribable. Everyone was carried away by it. Lucile was borne along, unresisting, by that strong torrent of enthusiasm; her interests, her objects, her ambitions, her husband, all were forgotten. His sentences grew longer, more rolling and sonorous. At length he reached the last of those cumulative periods which pile argument on argument as Pelion on Ossa. All pointed to an inevitable conclusion. The people saw it coming and when the last words fell, they were greeted with thunders of assent.

Then he sat down, drank some water, and pressed his hands to his head. The strain had been terrific. He was convulsed by his own emotions; every pulse in his body was throbbing, every nerve quivering; he streamed with perspiration and almost gasped for breath. For five minutes everyone shouted wildly; the delegates on the platform mounted their chairs and waved their arms. At his suggestion the great crowd would have sallied into the streets and marched on the palace; and it would have taken many bullets from the soldiers that Sorrento had so carefully posted to bring them back to the realisation of the squalid materialities of life.

The resolutions which Moret and Godoy proposed were carried by acclamation. Savrola turned to the former. "Well, Louis, I was right. How did it sound? I liked the last words. It is the best speech I have ever made."

Moret looked at him as at a god. "Splendid!" he said. "You have saved everything."

And now the meeting began to break up. Savrola walked to a side-door, and in a small waiting-room received the congratulations of all his principal supporters and friends. Lucile was hurried along in the press. Presently there was a block. Two men, of foreign aspect, stood in front of her, speaking in low tones.

"Brave words, Karl," said one.

"Ah," said the other, "we must have deeds. He is a good tool to work with at present; the time will come when we shall need something sharper."

"He has great power."

"Yes, but he is not of us. He has no sympathy with the cause. What does he care about a community of goods?"

"For my part," said the first man with an ugly laugh, "I have always been more attracted by the idea of a community of wives."

"Well, that too is part of the great scheme of society."

"When you deal them out, Karl, put me down as part proprietor of the President's."

He chuckled coarsely. Lucile shuddered. Here were the influences behind and beneath the great Democrat of which her husband had spoken.

The human stream began to flow on again. Lucile was carried by a current down a side street which led to the doorway by which Savrola would leave the hall. A bright gas-lamp made everything plainly visible. At length he appeared at the top of the steps, at the foot of which his carriage had already drawn up to receive him. The narrow street was filled with the crowd; the pressure was severe.

"Louis, come with me," said Savrola to Moret; "you can drop me and take the carriage on." Like many highly-wrought minds he yearned for sympathy and praise at such a moment; and he knew he would get them from Moret.

The throng, on seeing him, surged forward. Lucile, carried off her feet, was pushed into a dark burly man in front of her. Chivalrous gallantry is not among the peculiar characteristics of excited democracy. Without looking round the man jobbed backwards with his elbow and struck her in the breast. The pain was intense; involuntarily she screamed.

"Gentlemen," cried Savrola, "a woman has been hurt; I heard her voice. Give room there!" He ran down the steps. The crowd opened out. A dozen eager and officious hands were extended to assist Lucile, who was paralysed with terror. She would be recognised; the consequences were too awful to be thought of.

"Bring her in here," said Savrola. "Moret, help me." He half carried, half supported her up the steps into the small waiting-room. Godoy, Renos, and half a dozen of the Democratic leaders, who had been discussing the speech, grouped themselves around her curiously. He placed her in a chair. "A glass of water," he said quickly. Somebody handed him one, and he turned to offer it to her. Lucile, incapable of speech or motion, saw no way of escape. He must recognise her. The ridicule, the taunts, the danger, all were plain to her. As she made a feeble effort with her hand to decline the water, Savrola looked hard at her through her thick veil. Suddenly he started, spilling the water he was holding out to her. He knew her then! Now it would come—a terrible exposure!

"Why, Mirette," he cried, "my little niece! How could you come alone to such a crowded place at night? To hear my speech? Godoy, Renos, this is indeed a tribute! This means more to me than all the cheers of the people. Here is my sister's daughter who has risked the crowd to come and hear me speak. But your mother," he turned to Lucile, "should never have allowed you; this is no place for a girl alone. I must take you home. You are not hurt? If you had asked me, I could have ensured a seat for you out of the crowd. Is my carriage there? Good, we had better get home at once; your mother will be very anxious. Good-night, gentlemen. Come, my dear." He offered her his arm and led her down the steps. The people who filled the street, their upturned faces pale in the gas-light, cheered wildly. He put her into his carriage. "Drive on, coachman," he said, getting in himself.

"Where to, Sir?" asked the man.

Moret advanced to the carriage. "I will go on the box," he said. "I can take the carriage on after dropping you," and before Savrola could say a word he had climbed on to the seat beside the driver.

"Where to, Sir?" repeated the coachman.

"Home," said Savrola desperately.

The carriage started, passed through the cheering crowds, and out into the less frequented parts of the city.

CHAPTER XI.

IN THE WATCHES OF THE NIGHT.

Lucile lay back in the cushions of the brougham with a feeling of intense relief. He had saved her. An emotion of gratitude filled her mind, and on the impulse of the moment she took his hand and pressed it. It was the third time in their renewed acquaintance that their hands had met, and each time the significance had been different.

Savrola smiled. "It was most imprudent of your Excellency to venture into a crowd like that. Luckily I thought of an expedient in time. I trust you were not hurt in the throng?"

"No," said Lucile; "a man struck me with his elbow and I screamed. I should never have come."

"It was dangerous."

"I wanted to——" She paused.

"To hear me speak," he added, finishing her sentence for her.

"Yes; to see you use your power."

"I am flattered by the interest you take in me."

"Oh, it was on purely political grounds."

There was the suspicion of a smile on her face. He looked at her quickly. What did she mean? Why should it be necessary to say so? Her mind had contemplated another reason, then.

"I hope you were not bored," he said.

"It is terrible to have power like that," she replied earnestly; and then after a pause, "Where are we going to?"

"I would have driven you to the palace," said Savrola, "but our ingenuous young friend on the box has made it necessary that we should keep up this farce for a little longer. It will be necessary to get rid of him. For the present you had best remain my niece."

She looked up at him with an amused smile, and then said seriously: "It was brilliant of you to have thought of it, and noble of you to have carried it out. I shall never forget it; you have done me a great service."

"Here we are," said Savrola at length, as the brougham drew up at the entrance of his house. He opened the carriage-door; Moret jumped off the box and rang the bell. After a pause the old housekeeper opened the door. Savrola called to her. "Ah, Bettine, I am glad you are up. Here is my niece, who has been to the meeting to hear me speak and has been jostled by the crowd. I shall not let her go home alone to-night. Have you a bedroom ready?"

"There is the spare room on the first floor," answered the old woman; "but I fear that would never do."

"Why not?" asked Savrola quickly.

"Because the sheets for the big bed are not aired, and since the chimney was swept there has been no fire there."

"Oh, well, you must try and do what you can. Good-night, Moret. Will you send the carriage back as soon as you have done with it? I have some notes to send to THE RISING TIDE office about the articles for to-morrow morning. Don't forget,—as quickly as you can, for I am tired out."

"Good-night," said Moret. "You have made the finest speech of your life. Nothing can stop us while we have you to lead the way."

He got into the carriage and drove off. Savrola and Lucile ascended the stairs to the sitting-room, while the housekeeper bustled off to make preparations for the airing of sheets and pillow-cases. Lucile looked round the room with interest and curiosity. "I am in the heart of the enemy's camp now," she said.

"You will be in many hearts during your life," said Savrola, "whether you remain a queen or not."

"You are still determined to drive us out?"

"You heard what I said to-night."

"I ought to hate you," said Lucile; "and yet I don't feel that we are enemies."

"We are on opposite sides," he replied.

"Only politics come between us."

"Politics and persons," he added significantly, using a hackneyed phrase.

She looked at him with a startled glance. What did he mean? Had he read deeper into her heart than she herself had dared to look? "Where does that door lead to?" she asked irrelevantly.

"That? It leads to the roof,—to my observatory."

"Oh show it me," she cried. "Is it there you watch the stars?"

"I often look at them. I love them; they are full of suggestions and ideas."

He unlocked the door and led the way up the narrow winding stairs on to the platform. It was, as is usual in Laurania, a delicious night. Lucile walked to the parapet and looked over; all the lamps of the town twinkled beneath, and above were the stars.

Suddenly, far out in the harbour, a broad white beam of light shot out; it was the search-light of a warship. For a moment it swept along the military mole and rested on the battery at the mouth of the channel. The fleet was leaving the port, and picking its way through the difficult passage.

Savrola had been informed of the approaching departure of the admiral, and realised at once the meaning of what he saw. "That," he said, "may precipitate matters."

"You mean that when the ships are gone you will no longer fear to rise?"

"I do not fear; but it is better to await a good moment."

"And that moment?"

"Is perhaps imminent. I should like you to leave the capital. It will be no place for women in a few days. Your husband knows it; why has he not sent you away to the country?"

"Because," she replied, "we shall suppress this revolt, and punish those who have caused it."

"Have no illusions," said Savrola. "I do not miscalculate. The army cannot be trusted; the fleet is gone; the people are determined. It will not be safe for you to stay here."

"I will not be driven out," she answered with energy; "nothing shall make me fly. I will perish with my husband."

"Oh, we shall try to be much more prosaic than that," he said. "We shall offer a very handsome pension to the President, and he will retire with his beautiful wife to some gay and peaceful city, where he can enjoy life without depriving others of liberty."

"You think you can do all this?" she cried. "Your power can rouse the multitude; but can you restrain them?" And she told him of the words she had heard in the crowd that night. "Are you not playing with mighty forces?"

"Yes, I am," he said; "and that is why I have asked you to go away to the country for a few days, until things become settled one way or the other. It is possible that either I or your husband will go down. I shall of course try to save him, if we are successful; but, as you say, there are other forces which may be beyond control; and if he gets the upper hand——"

56

"Well?"

"I suppose I should be shot."

"Fearful!" she said. "Why will you persist?"

"Oh, it is only now, when the play is growing high, that I begin to appreciate the game. Besides, death is not very terrible."

"Afterwards may be."

"I do not think so. Life, to continue, must show a balance of happiness. Of one thing I feel sure; we may say of a future state,—'If any, then better.'"

"You apply your knowledge of this world to all others."

"Why not?" he said. "Why should not the same laws hold good all over the universe, and, if possible, beyond it? Other suns show by their spectra that they contain the same elements as ours."

"You put your faith in the stars," she said doubtingly, "and think, though you will not admit it, they can tell you everything."

"I never accused them of being interested in our concerns; but if they were, they might tell strange tales. Supposing they could read our hearts for instance?"

She glanced up and met his eye. They looked at each other hard. She gasped; whatever the stars might know, they had read each other's secret.

There was a noise of someone running up-stairs. It was the housekeeper.

"The carriage has returned," said Savrola in a quiet voice. "It can now take you back to the palace."

The old woman stepped out on to the roof, breathing hard from her climb. "I have aired the sheets," she said with exultation in her voice, "and the fire is burning brightly. There is some soup ready for the young lady, if she will come and take it, before it gets cold."

The interruption was so commonplace that both Lucile and Savrola laughed. It was a happy escape from an awkward moment. "You always manage, Bettine," he said, "to make everyone comfortable; but after all the bedroom will not be needed. My niece is afraid lest her mother be alarmed at her absence, and I am going to send her back in the carriage so soon as it returns."

The poor old soul looked terribly disappointed; the warm sheets, the cosy fire, the hot soup were comforts she loved to prepare for others, enjoying them, as it were, by proxy. She turned away and descended the narrow staircase mournfully, leaving them again alone.

So they sat and talked, not as before, but with full knowledge of their sympathy, while the moon climbed higher in the sky and the soft breezes stirred the foliage of the palm-trees in the garden below. Neither thought much of the future, nor did they blame the coachman's delay.

At length the silence of the night, and the train of their conversation were broken by the noise of wheels on the stony street.

"At last," said Savrola without enthusiasm. Lucile rose and looked over the parapet. A carriage approached almost at a gallop. It stopped suddenly at the door, and a man jumped out in a hurry. The door-bell rang loudly.

Savrola took both her hands. "We must part," he said; "when shall we meet again,—Lucile?"

She made no answer, nor did the moonlight betray the expression of her features. Savrola led the way down the stairs. As he entered the sitting-room, the further door was opened hastily by a man who, seeing Savrola, stopped short, and respectfully took off his hat. It was Moret's servant.

With considerable presence of mind Savrola shut the door behind him, leaving Lucile in the darkness of the staircase. She waited in astonishment; the door was thin. "My master, Sir," said a stranger's voice, "bade me bring you this with all speed and give it direct into your hand." There followed the tearing of paper, a pause, an exclamation, and then Savrola, in a voice steady with the steadiness which betrays intense emotion under control, replied: "Thank you very much; say I shall await them here. Don't take the carriage; go on foot,—stay, I will let you out myself."

She heard the other door open and the sound of their footsteps going down-stairs; then she turned the handle and entered. Something had happened, something sudden, unexpected, momentous. His voice,—strange how well she was beginning to know it!— had told her that. An envelope lay on the floor; on the table,—the table where the cigarette-box and the revolver lay side by side,—was a paper, half curled up as if anxious to preserve its secret.

Subtle, various, and complex are the springs of human action. She felt the paper touched her nearly; she knew it concerned him. Their interests were antagonistic; yet she did not know whether it was for his sake or her own that she was impelled to indulge a wild curiosity. She smoothed the paper out. It was brief and in a hurried hand, but to the point: Code wire just received says, Strelitz crossed frontier this morning with two thousand men and is marching hither via Turga and Lorenzo. The hour has come. I have sent to Godoy and Renos and will bring them round at once. Yours through hell, MORET.

Lucile felt the blood run to her heart; already she imagined the sound of musketry. It was true the hour had come. The fatal paper fascinated her; she could not take her eyes

58

from it. Suddenly the door opened and Savrola came in. The noise, her agitation, and above all the sense of detection wrung from her a low, short, startled scream. He grasped the situation immediately. "Bluebeard," he said ironically.

"Treason," she retorted taking refuge in furious anger. "So you will rise and murder us in the night,—conspirator!"

Savrola smiled suavely; his composure was again perfect. "I have sent the messenger away on foot, and the carriage is at your disposal. We have talked long; it is now three o'clock; your Excellency should not further delay your return to the palace. It would be most imprudent; besides, as you will realise, I expect visitors."

His calmness maddened her. "Yes," she retorted; "the President will send you some,—police."

"He will not know about the invasion yet."

"I shall tell him," she replied.

Savrola laughed softly. "Oh no," he said, "that would not be fair."

"All's fair in love and war."

"And this——?"

"Is both," she said, and then burst into tears.

After that they went down-stairs. Savrola helped her into the carriage. "Good-night," he said, though it was already morning, "and good-bye."

But Lucile, not knowing what to say or think or do, continued to cry inconsolably and the carriage drove away. Savrola closed the door and returned to his room. He did not feel his secret was in any danger.

CHAPTER XII.

A COUNCIL OF WAR.

Savrola had scarcely time to smoke a cigarette before the Revolutionary leaders began to arrive. Moret was the first; he rang the bell violently, stamping about on the doorstep till it was answered, ran upstairs three steps at a time, and burst impetuously into the room, aquiver with excitement. "Ah," he cried, "the hour has come,—not words but deeds now! We draw the sword in a good cause; for my part I shall fling away the scabbard; Fortune is on our side."

59

"Yes," said Savrola; "have some whisky and soda-water,—on the sideboard there. It is a good drink to draw the sword on,—the best in fact."

Moret somewhat abashed turned and walking to the table began opening a soda-water bottle. As he poured out the spirit the clinking of glass and bottle betrayed his agitation. Savrola laughed softly. Turning swiftly, his impetuous follower sought to hide his agitation by a fresh outburst. "I have told you throughout," he said, holding his glass on high, "that force was the only solution. It has come, as I predicted. I drink to it,—war, civil war, battle, murder, and sudden death,—by these means liberty will be regained!"

"Wonderful soothing effect these cigarettes have. There's no opium in them either,—soft, fresh Egyptians. I get them every week from Cairo. A little, old man I met there three years ago makes them,—Abdullah Rachouan."

He held out the box. Moret took one; the business of lighting it steadied him; he sat down and began to smoke furiously. Savrola watched him in dreamy calmness, looking often at the smoke-wreathes that rose about him. Presently he spoke. "So you are glad there is to be war and that people are to be killed?"

"I am glad that this tyranny is to be ended."

"Remember that we pay for every pleasure and every triumph we have in this world."

"I will take my chance."

"I trust, I would be glad if I could say with conviction, I pray, that the lot may not fall on you. But it is true nevertheless that we must pay, and for all the good things in life men pay in advance. The principles of sound finance apply."

"How do you mean?" asked Moret.

"Would you rise in the world? You must work while others amuse themselves. Are you desirous of a reputation for courage? You must risk your life. Would you be strong morally or physically? You must resist temptations. All this is paying in advance; that is prospective finance. Observe the other side of the picture; the bad things are paid for afterwards."

"Not always."

"Yes, as surely as the headache of Sunday morning follows the debauch of Saturday night, as an idle youth is requited by a barren age, as a gluttonous appetite promotes an ungainly paunch."

"And you think I shall have to pay for this excitement and enthusiasm? You think I have paid nothing so far?"

"You will have to take risks, that is paying. Fate will often throw double or quits. But on these hazards men should not embark with levity; the gentleman will always think of settling-day."

Moret was silent. Brave and impetuous as he was, the conversation chilled him. His was not the courage of the Stoic; he had not schooled himself to contemplate the shock of dissolution. He fixed his thoughts on the struggles and hopes of the world, as one might look at the flowers and grasses that were growing on the edge of a precipice towards which he was being impelled.

They remained for a few moments without speaking, till Godoy and Renos entered, having arrived simultaneously.

Each man of the four had taken the news, which meant so much to them, according to their natures. Savrola had put on the armour of his philosophy, and gazed on the world as from a distance. Moret had been convulsed with excitement. The other two, neither composed nor elated by the proximity and the approach of danger, showed that they were not the men for stirring times.

Savrola greeted them amiably, and all sat down. Renos was crushed. The heavy hammer of action had fallen on the delicate structures of precedent and technicality in which he had always trusted, and smashed them flat. Now that the crisis had arrived, the law, his shield and buckler, was first of all to be thrown away. "Why has he done this?" he asked. "What right had he to come without authorisation? He has committed us all. What can we do?"

Godoy too was shocked and frightened. He was one of those men who fear danger, who shrink from it, but yet embark deliberately on courses which they know must lead to it. He had long foreseen the moment of revolt, but had persisted in going on. Now it was upon him, and he trembled; still, his dignity strengthened him.

"What is to be done, Savrola?" he asked, turning instinctively to the greater soul and stronger mind.

"Well," said the leader, "they had no business to come without my orders; they have, as Renos has observed, committed us, while our plans are in some respects incomplete. Strelitz has disobeyed me flatly; I will settle with him later. For the present, recriminations are futile; we have to deal with the situation. The President will know of the invasion in the morning; some of the troops here will, I take it, be ordered to strengthen the Government forces in the field. Perhaps the Guard will be sent. I think the others would refuse to march; they are thoroughly in sympathy with the Cause. If so we must strike, much as we have arranged. You, Moret, will call the people to arms. The Proclamation must be printed, the rifles served out, the Revolution proclaimed. All the Delegates must be notified. If the soldiers fraternise, all will be well; if not, you will have to fight—I don't think there will be much opposition—storm the palace and make Molara prisoner."

"It shall be done," said Moret.

"Meanwhile," continued Savrola, "we will proclaim the Provisional Government at the Mayoralty. Thence I shall send you orders; thither you must send me reports. All this will happen the day after to-morrow."

Godoy shivered, but assented. "Yes," he said; "it is the only course, except flight and ruin."

"Very well; now we will go into details. First of all, the Proclamation. I will write that to-night. Moret, you must get it printed; you shall have it at six o'clock to-morrow morning. Then prepare the arrangements we had devised for assembling and arming the people; wait till you get a written order from me to put them into action. You, Renos, must see the members of the Provisional Government. Have the constitution of the Council of Public Safety printed, and be ready to circulate it to-morrow night; yet again, wait till I give the word. Much depends on the attitude of the troops; but everything is really ready. I do not think we need fear the result."

The intricate details of the plot, for plot it was, were well known to the leaders of the revolt. For several months they had looked to force as the only means of ending the government they detested. Savrola was not the man to commit himself to such an enterprise without taking every precaution. Nothing had been forgotten; the machinery of revolution only needed setting in motion. Yet in spite of the elaborate nature of the conspiracy and its great scale, the President and his police had been able to learn nothing definite. They feared that a rising was imminent; they had realised the danger for some months; but it was impossible to know where the political agitation ended, and the open sedition began. The great social position and almost European reputation of the principal leaders had rendered their arrest without certain proof a matter of extreme difficulty. The President, believing that the people would not rise unless spurred thereto by some act of power on the part of the Executive, feared to rouse them. But for this Savrola, Moret, and the others would have already filled cells in the State Prison; indeed, they would have had much to be thankful for had their lives been spared.

But Savrola understood his position, and had played his game with consummate tact and skill. The great parade he made of the political agitation had prevented the President from observing the conspiracy to deliberate violence which lay beneath. At length the preparations were approaching completion. It had become only a matter of days; Strelitz's impetuous act had but precipitated the course of events. One corner of the great firework had caught light too soon; it was necessary to fire the rest lest the effect should be spoiled.

He continued to go over the details of the scheme for nearly an hour, to make sure that there should be no mistakes. At last all was finished, and the members of the embryo Council of Public Safety took their departure. Savrola let them out himself, not wishing to wake the old nurse. Poor soul, why should she feel the force of the struggles of ambitious men?

Moret went off full of enthusiasm; the others were gloomy and preoccupied. Their great leader shut the door, and once more that night climbed the stairs to his chamber.

As he reached it, the first streaks of morning came in through the parted curtains of the windows. The room, in the grey light with its half-empty glasses and full ashtrays, looked like a woman, no longer young, surprised by an unsympathetic dawn in the meretricious paints and pomps of the previous night. It was too late to go to bed; yet he was tired, weary with that dry kind of fatigue which a man feels when all desire of sleep has passed away. He experienced a sensation of annoyance and depression. Life seemed unsatisfactory; something was lacking. When all deductions had been made on the scores of ambition, duty, excitement, or fame, there remained an unabsorbed residuum of pure emptiness. What was the good of it all? He thought of the silent streets; in a few hours they would echo with the crackle of musketry. Poor broken creatures would be carried bleeding to the houses, whose doors terrified women would close in the uncharitable haste of fear. Others, flicked out of human ken from solid concrete earth to unknown, unformulated abstractions, would lie limp and reproachful on the paving-stones. And for what? He could not find an answer to the question. The apology for his own actions was merged in the much greater apology nature would have to make for the existence of the human species. Well, he might be killed himself; and as the thought occurred to him he looked forward with a strange curiosity to that sudden change, with perhaps its great revelation. The reflection made him less dissatisfied with the shallow ends of human ambition. When the notes of life ring false, men should correct them by referring to the tuning-fork of death. It is when that clear menacing tone is heard that the love of life grows keenest in the human heart.

All men, from such moods and reflections, are recalled to earth by hard matters of fact. He remembered the proclamation he had to write, and rising plunged into the numerous details of the business of living, and thus forgot the barrenness of life. So he sat and wrote, while the pale glimmer of the dawn glowed into the clear light of sunrise and the warm tints of broad day.

CHAPTER XIII.

THE ACTION OF THE EXECUTIVE.

The private breakfast-room of the Presidential palace was a small but lofty apartment. The walls were hung with tapestries; over the doors weapons of ancient type and history were arranged in elaborate patterns. The great French windows were deeply set in the wall, and the bright light of the morning was softened by heavy crimson curtains. Like the rest of the house it wore an official aspect. The windows opened on to the stone terrace, and those who passed through them experienced a feeling of relief in exchanging the severe splendours of the palace for the beautiful confusion of the garden, where between the spreading trees and slender palms the sparkling waters of the harbour were displayed.

The table, which was set for two, was comfortably small and well arranged. The generous revenue which it had long been the principle of the Lauranian Republic to bestow on her First Magistrate enabled the President to live in a style of elegance and luxury, and to enjoy the attractions of good silver, fresh-cut flowers, and an excellent cook. But it was with a clouded brow that Molara met his wife at breakfast on the morning after the events which have just been chronicled.

"Bad news,—tiresome news again, dear," he said as, sitting down and depositing a handful of papers on the table, he signed to the servants to leave the room.

Lucile experienced a feeling of intense relief. After all she would not have to tell him the secret she had learned. "Has he started?" she asked incautiously.

"Yes, last night; but he will be stopped."

"Thank heaven for that!"

Molara looked at her in amazement.

"What do you mean? Why are you glad that the Admiral and the fleet are prevented from carrying out my orders?"

"The fleet!"

"Good gracious! What did you think I meant?" he asked impatiently.

A loophole of escape presented itself. She ignored his question. "I am glad the fleet is stopped because I think they will be wanted here, now that the city is so unsettled."

"Oh," said the President shortly,—suspiciously, she thought. To cover her retreat she asked a question. "Why are they stopped?"

Molara pulled out a Press telegram slip from among his papers.

"Port Said, September 9th, 6.0 a.m.," he said, reading; "British steam-collier Maude, 1,400 tons, grounded this morning in canal, which is in consequence blocked for traffic. Every effort is being made to clear the fairway. Accident is believed to be due to the silting up of channel caused by extreme draught of H.B.M.S. Aggressor which passed through last night." He added: "They know their business, these English pigs."

"You think they have done it on purpose?"

"Of course."

"But the fleet is not there yet."

"It will be there to-morrow night."

"But why should they block the channel now,—why not wait?"

"Characteristic dislike of coups de théâtre, I suppose. Now the French would have waited till we were at the entrance of the channel, and then shut the door in our faces neatly. But British Diplomacy does not aim at effects; besides, this looks more natural."

"How abominable!"

"And listen to this," said the President, as giving way to keen irritation he snatched another paper from his bundle and began to read. "From the Ambassador," he said: "Her Majesty's Government have instructed the officers commanding the various British coaling-stations south of the Red Sea, to render every assistance to the Lauranian fleet and to supply them with coal at the local market-rate."

"It is an insult," she said.

"It is a cat playing with a mouse," he rejoined bitterly.

"What will you do?"

"Do? Sulk, protest,—but give in. What else can we do? Their ships are on the spot; ours are cut off."

There was a pause. Molara read his papers and continued his breakfast. Lucile came back to her resolution. She would tell him; but she would make terms. Savrola must be protected at all costs. "Antonio," she said nervously.

The President, who was in a thoroughly bad temper, went on reading for a moment and then looked up abruptly. "Yes?"

"I must tell you something."

"Well, what is it?"

"A great danger is threatening us."

"I know that," he said shortly.

"Savrola———" She paused uncertain and undecided.

"What of him?" said Molara, suddenly becoming interested.

"If you were to find him guilty of conspiracy, of plotting revolution, what would you do?"

"I should shoot him with the greatest pleasure in the world."

"What, without a trial?"

"Oh no! He should have a trial under martial law and welcome. What of him?"

It was a bad moment. She looked round for another loophole.

"He—he made a speech last night," she said.

65

"He did," said the President impatiently.

"Well, I think it must have been very inflammatory, because I heard the crowds cheering in the streets all night."

Molara looked at her in deep disgust. "My dear, how silly you are this morning," he said and returned to his paper.

The long silence that followed was broken by the hurried entrance of Miguel with an opened telegram. He walked straight up to the President and handed it to him without speaking; but Lucile could see that he was trembling with haste, excitement, or terror.

Molara opened the folded paper leisurely, smoothed it on the table and then jumped out of his chair as he read it. "Good God! when did this come?"

"This moment."

"The fleet," he cried, "the fleet, Miguel,—not an instant must be lost! Recall the Admiral! They must return at once. I will write the telegram myself." Crumpling the message in his hand he hurried out of the room, Miguel at his heels. At the door he found a waiting servant. "Send for Colonel Sorrento,—to come here immediately. Go! be off! Run!" he cried as the man departed with ceremonious slowness.

Lucile heard them bustle down the corridor and the slam of a distant door; then all was silent again. She knew what that telegram contained. The tragedy had burst upon them all, that tragedy whose climax must strike her so nearly; but she felt glad she had meant to tell her husband,—and yet more glad that she had not told him. A cynic might have observed that Savrola's confidence, in the safety of his secret, was well founded.

She returned to her sitting-room. The uncertainty of the immediate future terrified her. If the revolt succeeded, she and her husband would have to fly for their lives; if it were suppressed the consequences seemed more appalling. One thing was clear: the President would send her out of the capital at once to some place of safety. Whither? Amid all these doubts and conflicting emotions one desire predominated,—to see Savrola again, to bid him good-bye, to tell him she had not betrayed him. It was impossible. A prey to many apprehensions she walked aimlessly about the room, awaiting the developements she feared.

Meanwhile the President and his secretary had reached the private office. Miguel shut the door. Both looked at each other.

"It has come," said Molara with a long breath.

"In an evil hour," replied the Secretary.

"I shall win, Miguel. Trust to my star, my luck,—I will see this thing through. We shall crush them; but much is to be done. Now write this telegram to our agent at Port Said; send it in cipher and clear the line: Charter at once fast despatch-boat and go

66

personally to meet Admiral de Mello, who with fleet left Laurania midnight 8th instant for Port Said. Stop. Order him in my name return here urgent. Stop. Spare no expense. Now send that off. With good luck the ships should be here to-morrow night."

Miguel sat down and began to put the message into code. The President paced the room excitedly; then he rang the bell; a servant entered.

"Has Colonel Sorrento come yet?"

"No, Your Excellency."

"Send and tell him to come at once."

"He has been sent for, Your Excellency."

"Send again."

The man disappeared.

Molara rang the bell once more. He met the servant in the doorway.

"Is there a mounted orderly?"

"Yes, Your Excellency."

"Finished, Miguel?"

"Here," said the Secretary, getting up and handing the message to the startled attendant,—"at speed."

"Go on," shouted the President, striking the table with his open hand, and the man fled from the room. The sound of the galloping horse somewhat allayed Molara's impatience.

"He crossed the frontier last night at nine o'clock, Miguel; he should have been at Turga at daybreak. We have a garrison there, a small one, but enough to delay the advance. Why is there no news? This telegram comes from Paris, from the Foreign Minister. We should have heard from—who is it commands the post?"

"I don't know, Your Excellency. The Colonel will be here directly; but the silence is ugly."

The President set his teeth. "I cannot trust the army; they are all disaffected. It is a terrible game; but I shall win, I shall win!" He repeated the sentence to himself several times with more energy than conviction, as if to fortify his heart.

The door opened. "Colonel Sorrento," announced the usher.

"Look here, old man," said Molara familiarly,—he felt he wanted a friend rather than a subordinate—"Strelitz has invaded us. He crossed the frontier last night with two thousand men and several Maxim guns, marching here by Turga and Lorenzo. We have no news from the Commandant at Turga; who is he?"

Sorrento was one of those soldiers, not an uncommon type, who fear little but independent responsibility. He had served under the President for many years in the field and in the Government. Had he been alone when the news arrived, he would have been thunderstruck; now that he had a leader he followed and obeyed with military precision. Without any appearance of surprise he thought for a moment and then replied: "Major de Roc. He has four companies,—a good officer,—you can trust him, Sir."

"But the troops?"

"That's another matter altogether. The whole army, as I have several times informed you, Sir, is disturbed. Only the Guard can be relied on, and, of course, the officers."

"Well, we shall see," said the President stoutly. "Miguel, get the map. You know the country, Sorrento. Between Turga and Lorenzo, the Black Gorge must be held. Here," he pointed on the map, which the Secretary unrolled, "here they must be stopped or at any rate delayed, till the fleet comes back. What is there at Lorenzo?"

"A battalion and two machine-guns," replied the War-Minister.

The President took a turn up and down the room. He was used to deciding quickly. "A brigade would do it for certain," he said. He took another turn. "Rail two battalions of the Guard at once to Lorenzo." Sorrento, who had produced his note-book, began to write. "Two field-batteries," said the President. "Which two are fit, Colonel?"

"The first and second will do," answered Sorrento.

"And the Lancers of the Guard."

"All?"

"Yes, all, except details for orderly-work."

"That leaves you only one trustworthy battalion."

"I know," said the President. "It is a bold course, but the only one. Now what about the Line regiments in the city? Which are the worst?"

"The third, fifth, and eleventh have caused us most uneasiness."

"Very well; we will get them out of the way. Let them march to-day towards Lorenzo and halt anywhere ten miles out of the city as a supporting brigade. Now, who is to command?"

"Rollo is senior, Sir."

68

"A fool, a fossil, and out of date," cried the President.

"Stupid, but steady," said Sorrento. "You can rely upon his attempting nothing brilliant; he will do what he is told, and nothing more."

Molara reflected on this tremendous military virtue. "Very well; give him the supporting brigade; they will have no fighting. But the other business; that is different. Brienz should have it."

"Why not Drogan?" suggested the War-Minister.

"I can't stand his wife," said the President.

"He is a good musician, Sir," interposed Miguel.

"Guitar,—very melodious." He shook his head appreciatively.

"And has a capital cook," added Sorrento.

"No," said Molara; "this is a matter of life and death. I cannot indulge my prejudices, nor yours; he is not a good man."

"A good Staff would run him all right, Sir; he is very placid and easily led. And he is a great friend of mine; many's the good dinner——"

"No, Colonel, it's no good; I cannot. Is it likely that when so much is at stake, when my reputation, my chances in life, indeed life itself, are on the hazard, that I or any one would give a great command on such grounds? If claims were equally balanced, I would oblige you; but Brienz is a better man and must have it. Besides," he added, "he has not got a horrid wife." Sorrento looked terribly disappointed but said no more. "Well, that is all settled. I leave all details to you. The Staff, everything, you may appoint; but the troops must start by noon. I will speak to them myself at the station."

The War-Minister bowed and departed, solaced by the minor appointments which the President had left to his decision.

Molara looked at his secretary dubiously. "Is there anything else to do? None of the revolutionaries in the city have moved, have they?"

"They have given no sign, Sir; there is nothing to incriminate them."

"It is possible this has surprised them; their plans are not ready. At the first overt act of violence or sedition, I will arrest them. But I must have proofs, not for my own satisfaction, but for the country."

"This is a critical moment," said the Secretary. "If the leaders of the sedition could be discredited, if they could be made to appear ridiculous or insincere, it would have a great effect on public opinion."

"I had thought," replied Molara, "that we might hope to learn something of their plans."

"You have informed me that Her Excellency has consented to ask Señor Savrola for information on this point?"

"I dislike the idea of any intimacy between them; it might be dangerous."

"It might be made most dangerous for him."

"In what way?"

"In the way I have already indicated to you, General."

"Do you mean in the way I forbade you to suggest, Sir?"

"Certainly."

"And this is the moment?"

"Now or never."

There was a silence, after which they resumed the morning's business. For an hour and a half both worked busily. Then Molara spoke. "I hate doing it; it's a dirty job."

"What is necessary, is necessary," said the Secretary sententiously. The President was about to make a reply when a clerk entered the room with a deciphered telegram. Miguel took it from him, read it, and passed it to his chief, saying grimly as he did so: "Perhaps this will decide you."

The President read the message, and as he read his face grew hard and cruel. It was from the Police Commissary at Turga, brief but terrible; the soldiers had deserted to the invaders, having first shot their officers.

"Very well," said Molara at last, "I shall require you to accompany me to-night on a mission of importance. I will take an aide-de-camp as well."

"Yes," said the Secretary; "witnesses are necessary."

"I shall be armed."

"That is desirable, but only as a threat, only as a threat," said the Secretary earnestly. "He is too strong for violence; the people would be up in a moment."

"I know that," curtly replied the President, and then with savage bitterness he added: "but for that there would be no difficulty."

"None whatever," said Miguel, and went on writing.

Molara rose and went in search of Lucile, choking down the disgust and repugnance he felt. He was determined now; it might just make the difference to him in the struggle for power, and besides, it contained the element of revenge. He would like to see the proud Savrola grovel and beg for mercy at his feet. All mere politicians, he said to himself, were physical cowards; the fear of death would paralyse his rival.

Lucile was still in her sitting-room when her husband entered. She met him with an anxious look. "What has happened, Antonio?"

"We have been invaded, dearest, by a large force of revolutionaries. The garrison of Turga have deserted to the enemy, and killed their officers. The end is now in sight."

"It is terrible," she said.

"Lucile," he said with unwonted tenderness, "one chance remains. If you could find out what the leaders of the agitation in this city intend to do, if you can get Savrola to show his hand, we might maintain our position and overcome our enemies. Can you,— will you do this?"

Lucile's heart bounded. It was, as he said, a chance. She might defeat the plot, and at the same time make terms for Savrola; she might still rule in Laurania, and, though this thought she repressed, save the man she loved. Her course was clear; to obtain the information and sell it to her husband for Savrola's life and liberty. "I will try," she said.

"I knew you would not fail me, dearest," said Molara. "But the time is short; go and see him to-night at his rooms. He will surely tell you. You have power over men and will succeed."

Lucile reflected. To herself she said, "I shall save the State and serve my husband;" and herself rejoined, "You will see him again." Then she spoke aloud. "I will go to-night."

"My dear, I always trusted you," said the President; "I will never forget your devotion."

Then he hurried away, convulsed with remorse,—and shame. He had indeed stooped to conquer.

CHAPTER XIV.

THE LOYALTY OF THE ARMY.

The military force of the Lauranian Republic was proportioned to the duties of protecting its territories from invasion and of maintaining law and order within them, but

71

was by the wisdom of former days restricted to limits which did not encourage great schemes of foreign conquest nor any aggressive meddling in the affairs of the neighbouring principalities. Four regiments of cavalry, twenty battalions of foot, and eight field-batteries comprised the Army of the Line. Besides these there was the Republican Guard, which consisted of a regiment of Lancers and three strong battalions of veteran infantry and supported by their discipline the authority, and by their magnificence the dignity, of the State.

The great capital city, which exceeded in wealth, population, and turbulence the aggregate of the provincial towns, had for its garrison the Guard and half of the entire army. The remaining troops were scattered in small country stations and on the frontiers.

All the pains that the President had taken to maintain the good will of the soldiery had proved vain. The revolutionary movement had grown apace in the ranks of the army, till they were now thoroughly disaffected, and the officers felt that their orders would be obeyed only so far as they were agreeable. With the Guard it was different. All, or nearly all, had borne their part in the late war and had marched to victory under the generalship of the President. They honoured and trusted their former commander, and were in turn honoured and trusted by him; indeed the favour he had shewn them may have been among the causes which had alienated the rest.

It was the greater part of this Guard that Molara, in his heavy need, was about to send against the invaders. He well knew the danger of depriving himself of the only troops he could rely on, should the city itself rise; but the advancing forces must be stopped at all hazards, and the Guard alone were able and willing to do the work. He would be left almost alone amid the populace who detested him, in the city he had ruled so sternly, with mutinous soldiers as his only defenders. It was not an inviting prospect, yet it presented some chances of success. It displayed a confidence which, though assumed, might decide the waverers and disgust his foes; and it dealt with the most pressing emergency, which was after all the first duty of the Executive. He did not doubt the ability of the troops he had despatched to disperse, if not to destroy, the rabble that had crossed the frontier. That danger at least was removed by his action. In two days the fleet would return, and under its guns his Government might still continue, feared and respected. The intervening period was the crisis, a crisis which he hoped to pass safely through, partly by the force of his personality, and partly by the ridicule and contempt in which he intended to plunge his terrible rival.

Punctually at eleven o'clock he left his private office to attire himself in his full uniform as a general of the army, in order that at the parade the troops might be reminded that he too was a soldier and one who had seen much war.

At the door Lieutenant Tiro presented himself, in a great state of perturbation. "Sir," he said, "you will allow me to go with my squadron to the front? There will be nothing for me to do here."

"On the contrary," replied the President, "there will be a great deal for you to do here. You must stay."

Tiro turned pale. "I do beg you, Sir, to allow me to go," he said earnestly.

72

"Impossible,—I want you here."

"But, Sir——"

"Oh, I know," said Molara impatiently; "you want to get shot at. Stay here, and I promise you shall hear bullets in plenty before you have done." He turned away, but the look of bitter disappointment on the young officer's face induced him to pause. "Besides," he added, assuming that charm of manner of which few great men are destitute, "I require you for a service of difficulty and extreme danger. You have been specially selected."

The Subaltern said no more, but he was only half consoled. He thought ruefully of the green country, the glinting lances, the crack of the rifles, and all the interest and joy of war. He would miss everything; his friends would be there, but he would not share their perils. They would talk of their adventures in after days and he would have no part in their discussions; they would even laugh at him as a "tame cat" of the palace, an aide-de-camp for ornamental purposes only. And as he mourned, a distant trumpet-call stung him like the cut of a whip. It was Boots and Saddles,—the Lancers of the Guard were turning out. The President hurried off to array himself, and Tiro descended the stairs to order the horses.

Molara was soon ready, and joined his aide-de-camp on the steps of the palace. Attended by a small escort they rode to the railway-station, passing, on the way, through groups of sullen citizens who stared insolently, and even spat on the ground in hatred and anger.

The artillery had already been despatched, but the entraining of the rest of the troops had not commenced when the President arrived, and they were drawn up (the cavalry in mass, the infantry in line of quarter-columns) in the open space in front of the terminus. Colonel Brienz, who commanded the force, was mounted at their head. He advanced and saluted; the band struck up the Republican Hymn, and the infantry presented arms with a clash of precision. The President acknowledged these compliments with punctilious care; and then, as the rifles were shouldered, he rode towards the ranks.

"You have a splendid force, Colonel Brienz," he said addressing the Colonel, but speaking loud enough to be heard by the troops. "To your skill and to their courage the Republic entrusts its safety, and entrusts it with confidence." He then turned to the troops: "Soldiers, some of you will remember the day I asked you to make a great effort for your country and your honour; Sorato is the name that history has given to the victory which was your answer to my appeal. Since then we have rested in peace and security, protected by the laurels that have crowned your bayonets. Now, as the years have passed, those trophies are challenged, challenged by the rabble whose backs you have seen so often. Take off the old laurels, soldiers of the Guard, and with the bare steel win new ones. Once again I ask you to do great things, and when I look along your ranks, I cannot doubt that you will do them. Farewell, my heart goes with you; would to God I were your leader!"

He shook hands with Brienz and with the senior officers amid loud cheers from the troops, some of whom broke from the ranks to press around him, while others raised

73

their helmets on their bayonets in warlike enthusiasm. But as the shouting ceased, a long, discordant howl of derision, till then drowned by the noise, was heard from the watching crowds,—a sinister comment!

Meanwhile at the other end of the town the mobilisation of the Reserve Brigade revealed the extreme contrast between the loyalty and discipline of the Guard and the disaffection of the regiments of the Line.

An ominous silence reigned throughout the barracks. The soldiers walked about moodily and sullenly, making little attempt to pack their kits for the impending march. Some loitered in groups about the parade-ground and under the colonnade which ran round their quarters; others sat sulking on their cots. The habit of discipline is hard to break, but here were men steeling themselves to break it.

These signs did not pass unnoticed by the officers who awaited in anxious suspense the hour of parade.

"Don't push them," Sorrento had said to the colonels, "take them very gently;" and the colonels had severally replied that they would answer with their lives for the loyalty of their men. It was nevertheless thought advisable to try the effect of the order upon a single battalion, and the 11th Regiment was the first to receive the command to turn out.

The bugles blew briskly and cheerily, and the officers, hitching up their swords and pulling on their gloves, hurried to their respective companies. Would the men obey the summons? It was touch and go. Anxiously they waited. Then by twos and threes the soldiers shuffled out and began to form up in their ranks. At length the companies were complete, sufficiently complete, that is to say, for there were many absentees. The officers inspected their units. It was a dirty parade; the accoutrements were uncleaned, the uniforms carelessly put on, and the general appearance of the men was slovenly to a degree. But of these things no notice was taken, and as they walked along the ranks the subalterns found something to say in friendly chaff to many of their soldiers. They were greeted however with a forbidding silence, a silence not produced by discipline or by respect. Presently Markers sounded, the companies moved to the general parade-ground, and soon the whole battalion was drawn up in the middle of the barrack-square.

The Colonel was on his horse, faultlessly attired, and attended by his Adjutant. He looked calmly at the solid ranks before him, and nothing in his bearing revealed the terrible suspense which filled his mind and gripped his nerve. The Adjutant cantered along the column collecting the reports. "All present, Sir," said the company commanders, but there were several whose voices quavered. Then he returned to the Colonel, and fell into his place. The Colonel looked at his regiment, and the regiment at their Colonel.

"Battalion,—attention!" he cried, and the soldiers sprang up with a clatter and a click. "Form,—fours."

The word of command was loud and clear. About a dozen soldiers moved at the call of instinct—moved a little—looked about them, and shuffled back to their places again. The rest budged not an inch. A long and horrid silence followed. The Colonel's face turned grey.

74

"Soldiers," he said, "I have given you an order; remember the honour of the regiment. Form,—fours." This time not a man moved. "As you were," he shouted desperately, though it was an unnecessary command. "The battalion will advance in quarter-column. Quick march!"

The battalion remained motionless.

"Captain Lecomte," said the Colonel, "what is the name of the right-hand man of your company?"

"Sergeant Balfe, Sir," replied the officer.

"Sergeant Balfe, I order you to advance. Quick—march!"

The sergeant quivered with excitement; but he held his ground.

The Colonel opened his pouch and produced his revolver with much deliberation. He looked carefully at it, as if to see that it was well cleaned; then he raised the hammer and rode up close to the mutineer. At ten yards he stopped and took aim. "Quick—march!" he said in a low menacing voice.

It was evident that a climax had been reached, but at this instant Sorrento, who, concealed in the archway of the barrack-gate, had watched the proceedings, rode into the square and trotted towards the soldiers. The Colonel lowered his pistol.

"Good-morning," said the War-Minister.

The officer replaced his weapon and saluted.

"Is the regiment ready to move off?" and then before a reply could be given he added: "A very smart parade, but after all it will not be necessary to march to-day. The President is anxious that the men should have a good night's rest before starting, and," raising his voice, "that they should drink a bumper to the Republic and confusion to her enemies. You may dismiss them, Colonel."

"Fall out," said the Colonel, not even caring to risk going through the correct procedure for dismissing.

The parade broke up. The ordered ranks dissolved in a crowd, and the soldiers streamed off towards their barracks. The officers alone remained.

"I should have shot him, Sir, in another instant," said the Colonel.

"No good," said Sorrento, "to shoot one man; it would only infuriate them. I will have a couple of machine-guns down here to-morrow morning, and we shall see then what will happen."

He turned suddenly, interrupted by a storm of broken and confused cheering. The soldiers had almost reached their barracks; one man was raised on the shoulders of others, and surrounded by the rest of the regiment, waving their helmets, brandishing their rifles, and cheering wildly.

"It is the sergeant," said the Colonel.

"So I perceive," replied Sorrento bitterly. "A popular man, I suppose. Have you many non-commissioned officers like that?" The Colonel made no reply. "Gentlemen," said the War-Minister to the officers who loitered on the square, "I would recommend you to go to your quarters. You are rather tempting targets here, and I believe your regiment is a particularly good shooting regiment. Is it not, Colonel?"

With which taunt he turned and rode away, sick at heart with anger and anxiety, while the officers of the 11th Regiment of Lauranian Infantry retired to their quarters to hide their shame and face their danger.

CHAPTER XV.

SURPRISES.

It had been a busy and exciting day for Savrola. He had seen his followers, had issued orders, restrained the impetuous, stimulated the weak, encouraged the timid. All day long messages and reports had reached him about the behaviour of the soldiers. The departure of the Guard, and the refusal of the supporting brigade to march, were equally pleasing events. The conspiracy had now been made known to so many persons that he doubted the possibility of keeping it much longer secret from the Government agents. From every consideration he felt that the hour had come. The whole of the elaborate plan that he had devised had been put into execution. The strain had been severe, but at length all the preparations were completed, and the whole strength of the Revolutionary party was concentrated for the final struggle. Godoy, Renos, and the others were collected at the Mayoralty, whence at dawn the Provisional Government was to be proclaimed. Moret, to whom the actual duty of calling the people to arms had been assigned, instructed his agents at his own house and made arrangements for the posting of the proclamation. All was ready. The leader on whom everything depended, whose brain had conceived, whose heart had inspired, the great conspiracy, lay back in his chair. He needed and desired a few moments' rest and quiet reflection to review his schemes, to look for omissions, to brace his nerves.

A small bright fire burned in the grate, and all around were the ashes of burnt papers. For an hour he had been feeding the flames. One phase of his life was over; there might be another, but it was well to have done with this one first. Letters from friends, dead now or alienated; letters of congratulation, of praise that had inspired his younger ambitions; letters from brilliant men and some from beautiful women,—all had met a common fate. Why should these records, be preserved for the curious eye of unsympathetic posterity? If he perished, the world might forget him, and welcome; if he lived, his life would henceforth be within the province of the historian. A single note, preserved from the general destruction, lay on the table beside him. It was the one with which Lucile had accompanied her invitation to the State Ball, the only one he had ever received from her.

As he balanced it in his fingers, his thoughts drifted away from the busy hard realities of life to that kindred soul and lovely face. That episode too was over. A barrier stood between them. Whatever the result of the revolt, she was lost to him, unless—and that terrible unless was pregnant with suggestions of such awful wickedness that his mind recoiled from it as a man's hand starts from some filthy thing he has by inadvertence touched. There were sins, sins against the commonwealth of mankind, against the phenomenon of life itself, the stigma of which would cling through death, and for which there was pardon only in annihilation. Yet he hated Molara with a fierce hatred; nor did he care to longer hide from himself the reason. And with the recollection of the reason his mind reverted to a softer mood. Would he ever see her again? Even the sound of her name pleased him; "Lucile," he whispered sadly.

There was a quick step outside; the door opened, and she stood before him. He sprang up in mute astonishment.

Lucile looked greatly embarrassed. Her mission was a delicate one. Indeed she did not know her own mind, or did not care to know it. It was for her husband's sake, she said to herself; but the words she spoke belied her. "I have come to tell you that I did not betray your secret."

"I know,—I never feared," replied Savrola.

"How do you know?"

"I have not yet been arrested."

"No, but he suspects."

"Suspects what?"

"That you are conspiring against the Republic."

"Oh!" said Savrola, greatly relieved; "he has no proofs."

"To-morrow he may have."

"To-morrow will be too late."

"Too late?"

"Yes," said Savrola; "the game begins to-night." He took out his watch; it was a quarter to eleven.

"At twelve o'clock you will hear the alarm-bells. Sit down, and let us talk."

Lucile sat down mechanically.

"You love me," he said in an even voice, looking at her dispassionately, and as if the whole subject of their relations was but a psychological problem, "and I love you." There was no answer; he continued: "But we must part. In this world we are divided, nor do I see how the barrier can be removed. All my life I shall think of you; no other woman can ever fill the empty space. Ambitions I still have: I always had them; but love I am not to know, or to know it only to my vexation and despair. I will put it away from me, and henceforth my affections will be as lifeless as those burnt papers. And you,—will you forget? In the next few hours I may be killed; if so, do not allow yourself to mourn. I do not care to be remembered for what I was. If I have done anything that may make the world more happy, more cheerful, more comfortable, let them recall the action. If I have spoken a thought which, rising above the vicissitudes of our existence, may make life brighter or death less gloomy, then let them say, 'He said this or he did that.' Forget the man; remember, perhaps, his work. Remember too that you have known a soul, somewhere amid the puzzles of the universe, the complement of your own; and then forget. Summon your religion to your aid; anticipate the moment of forgetting; live, and leave the past alone. Can you do this?"

"Never!" she answered passionately. "I will never forget you!"

"We are but poor philosophers," he said. "Pain and love make sport of us and all our theories. We cannot conquer ourselves or rise above our state."

"Why should we try?" she whispered, looking at him with wild eyes.

He saw and trembled. Then, with the surge of impulse, he cried, "My God, how I love you!" and before she could frame a resolution or even choose her mind, they had kissed each other.

The handle of the door turned quickly. Both started back. The door swung open and the President appeared. He was in plain clothes, his right hand concealed behind his back. Miguel followed from out of the darkness of the passage.

For a moment there was silence. Then Molara in a furious voice broke out: "So, Sir, you attack me in this way also,—coward and scoundrel!" He raised his hand and pointed the revolver it held full at his enemy.

Lucile, feeling that the world had broken up, fell back against the sofa, stunned with terror. Savrola rose and faced the President. Then she saw what a brave man he was, for as he did so he contrived to stand between the weapon and herself. "Put down your pistol," he said in a firm voice; "and you shall have an explanation."

"I will put it down," said Molara, "when I have killed you."

Savrola measured the distance between them with his eye. Could he spring in under the shot? Again he looked at the table where his own revolver lay. He shielded her, and he decided to stand still.

"Down on your knees and beg for mercy, you hound; down, or I will blow your face in!"

"I have always tried to despise death, and have always succeeded in despising you. I shall bow to neither."

"We shall see," said Molara, grinding his teeth. "I shall count five,—one!"

There was a pause. Savrola looked at the pistol barrel, a black spot encircled by a ring of bright steel; all the rest of the picture was a blank.

"Two!" counted the President.

So he was to die,—flash off this earth when that black spot burst into flame. He anticipated the blow full in his face; and beyond he saw nothing,—annihilation,—black, black night.

"Three!"

He could just see the rifling of the barrel; the lands showed faintly. That was a wonderful invention—to make the bullet spin as it travelled. He imagined it churning his brain with hideous energy. He tried to think, to take one grip of his philosophy or faith before the plunge; but his physical sensations were too violent. To the tips of his fingers he tingled, as the blood surged through his veins; the palms of his hands felt hot.

"Four!"

Lucile sprang up, and with a cry threw herself in front of the President "Wait, wait!" she cried. "Have mercy!"

Molara met her look, and in those eyes read more than terror. Then at last he understood; he started as though he had caught hold of red-hot iron. "My God! it's true!" he gasped. "Strumpet!" he cried, as he pushed her from him, striking her with the back of his left hand in the mouth. She shrank into the far corner of the room. He saw it all now. Hoist with his own petard he had lost everything. Wild fury took hold of him and shook him till his throat rattled and ached. She had deserted him; power was slipping from his grasp; his rival, his enemy, the man he hated with all his soul was everywhere triumphant. He had walked into the trap only to steal the bait; but he should not escape. There was a limit to prudence and to the love of life. His plans, his hopes, the roar of an avenging crowd, all faded from his mind. Death should wipe out the long score that stood between them, death which settled all,—now on the instant. But he had been a soldier, and was ever a practical man in the detail of life. He lowered the pistol and deliberately cocked it; single action would make certainty more sure; then he took good aim.

79

Savrola, seeing that the moment was upon him, lowered his head and sprang forward.

The President fired.

But Miguel's quick intelligence had appreciated the changed situation, and he remembered that there were consequences. He saw that the trick had become deadly earnest, and he did not forget the mob. He struck the pistol up, and the bullet, by a very little, flew high.

In the smoke and the flash Savrola closed with his adversary and bore him to the ground. Molara fell underneath and with the concussion dropped the revolver. The other seized it, wrenched himself clear, and sprang back and away from the prostrate figure. For a moment he stood there and watched, while the hungry lust of killing rose in his heart and made his trigger-finger itch. Then very slowly the President rose. The fall had dazed him; he leaned against the book-case and groaned.

Below there was a beating at the front door. Molara turned towards Lucile, who still cowered in the corner of the room, and began to revile her. The common, ugly material of his character showed through the veneer and polish that varied intercourse and the conduct of great affairs had superimposed. His words were not fit to hear, nor worth remembering; but they stung her to the quick and she rejoined defiantly: "You knew I was here; you told me to come! You have laid a trap; the fault is yours!" Molara replied by a filthy taunt. "I am innocent," she cried; "though I love him, I am innocent! Why did you tell me to come here?"

Savrola began to perceive dimly. "I do not know," he said, "what villainy you have contrived. I have wronged you too much to care to have your blood on my head; but go, and go quickly; I will not endure your foulness. Go!"

The President was now recovering his calmness. "I should have shot you myself," he said, "but I will have it done by a platoon of soldiers,—five soldiers and a corporal."

"The murder will be avenged in either case."

"Why did you stop me, Miguel?"

"It is as he says, Your Excellency," replied the Secretary. "It would have been a tactical error."

The official manner, the style of address, the man's composure, restored the President to his senses. He walked towards the door and stopping at the sideboard helped himself to a glass of brandy with ostentation. "Confiscated," he said, and held it up to the light, "by order of the Government." He swallowed it. "I will see you shot to-morrow," he added, heedless that the other held the pistol.

"I shall be at the Mayoralty," said Savrola; "you may come and fetch me if you dare."

"Revolt!" said the President. "Pooh! I will stamp it out, and you too, before the sun has gone down."

"Perhaps there may be another ending to the tale."

"One or the other," said the President. "You have robbed me of my honour; you are plotting to rob me of my power. There is not room for both of us in the world. You may take your mistress with you to hell."

There was a noise of hasty footsteps on the stairs; Lieutenant Tiro flung open the door, but stopped abruptly in astonishment at the occupants of the room. "I heard a shot," he said.

"Yes," answered the President; "there has been an accident, but luckily no harm was done. Will you please accompany me to the palace? Miguel, come!"

"You had better be quick, Sir," said the Subaltern. "There are many strange folk about to-night, and they are building a barricade at the end of the street."

"Indeed?" said the President. "It is time we took steps to stop them. Good-night, Sir," he added, turning to Savrola; "we shall meet to-morrow and finish our discussion."

But Savrola, revolver in hand, looked at him steadily and let him go in silence, a silence that for a space Lucile's sobs alone disturbed. At length, when the retreating footsteps had died away and the street door had closed, she spoke. "I cannot stop here."

"You cannot go back to the palace."

"What am I to do, then?"

Savrola reflected. "You had better stay here for the present. The house is at your disposal, and you will be alone. I must go at once to the Mayoralty; already I am late,—it is close on twelve,—the moment approaches. Besides, Molara will send policemen, and I have duties to discharge which I cannot avoid. To-night the streets are too dangerous. Perhaps I shall return in the morning."

The tragedy had stunned them both. A bitter remorse filled Savrola's heart. Her life was ruined,—was he the cause? He could not say how far he was guilty or innocent; but the sadness of it all was unaltered, no matter who might be at fault. "Good-bye," he said rising. "I must go, though I leave my heart behind. Much depends on me,—the lives of friends, the liberties of a nation."

And so he departed to play a great game in the face of all the world, to struggle for those ambitions which form the greater part of man's interest in life; while she, a woman, miserable and now alone, had no resource but to wait.

And then suddenly the bells began to ring all over the city with quick impatient strokes. There was the sound of a far-off bugle-call and a dull report,—the boom of an alarm-gun. The tumult grew; the roll of a drum beating the assembly was heard at the end of the street; confused shoutings and cries rose from many quarters. At length one sound was heard which put an end to all doubts,—tap, tap, tap, like the subdued slamming of many wooden boxes—the noise of distant musketry.

The revolution had begun.

CHAPTER XVI.

THE PROGRESS OF THE REVOLT.

Meanwhile the President and his two followers pursued their way through the city. Many people were moving about the streets, and here and there dark figures gathered in groups. The impression that great events were impending grew; the very air was sultry and surcharged with whisperings. The barricade, which was being built outside Savrola's house, had convinced Molara that a rising was imminent; half a mile from the palace the way was blocked by another. Three carts had been stopped and drawn across the street, and about fifty men were working silently to strengthen the obstruction: some pulled up the flat paving-stones; others were carrying mattresses and boxes filled with earth from the adjacent houses; but they paid little attention to the President's party. He turned up his collar and pressing his felt hat well down on his face clambered over the barrier,—the significance of what he saw filling his mind; the Subaltern indeed in his undress uniform drew some curious looks, but no attempt was made to stop his progress. These men waited for the signal.

All this time Molara said not a word. With the approach of danger he made great efforts to regain his calmness, that he might have a clear head to meet it; but for all his strength of will, his hatred of Savrola filled his mind to the exclusion of everything else. As he reached the palace the revolt broke out all over the city. Messenger after messenger hurried up with evil news. Some of the regiments had refused to fire on the people; others were fraternising with them; everywhere barricades grew and the approaches to the palace were on all sides being closed. The Revolutionary leaders had gathered at the Mayoralty. The streets were placarded with the Proclamation of the Provisional Government. Officers from various parts of the town hastened to the palace; some were wounded, many agitated. Among them was Sorrento, who brought the terrible news that an entire battery of artillery had surrendered their guns to the rebels. By half-past three it was evident, from the reports which were received by telegram and messenger, that the greater part of the city had passed into the hands of the Revolutionaries with very little actual fighting.

The President bore all with a calmness which revealed the full strength of his hard, stern character. He had, in truth, a terrible stimulant. Beyond the barricades and the rebels who lined them was the Mayoralty and Savrola. The face and figure of his enemy was before his eyes; everything else seemed of little importance. Yet he found in the blinding emergency an outlet for his fury, a counter-irritant for his grief; to crush the revolt, but above all to kill Savrola, was his heart's desire.

"We must wait for daylight," he said.

"And what then, Sir?" asked the War-Minister.

"We will then proceed to the Mayoralty and arrest the leaders of this disturbance."

The rest of the night was spent in organising a force with which to move at dawn. A few hundred faithful soldiers (men who had served with Molara in the former war), seventy officers of the regular army, whose loyalty was unquestionable, and the remaining battalion of the Guard with a detachment of armed police, were alone available. This band of devoted men, under fourteen hundred in number, collected in the open space in front of the palace-gates, and guarded the approaches while they waited for sunrise.

They were not attacked. "Secure the city," had been Savrola's order, and the rebels were busily at work on the barricades, which in a regular system rose on all sides. Messages of varied import continued to reach the President. Louvet, in a hurried note, expressed his horror at the revolt, and explained how much he regretted being unable to join the President at the palace. He had to leave the city in great haste, he said; a relative was dangerously ill. He adjured Molara to trust in Providence; for his part he was confident that the Revolutionaries would be suppressed.

The President in his room read this with a dry, hard laugh. He had never put the slightest faith in Louvet's courage, having always realised that in a crisis he would be useless and a coward. He did not blame him; the man had his good points, and as a public official in the Home-Office he was admirable; but war was not his province.

He passed the letter to Miguel. The Secretary read it and reflected. He also was no soldier. It was evident that the game was up, and there was no need for him to throw his life away, merely out of sentiment as he said to himself. He thought of the part he had played in the drama of the night. That surely gave him some claims; it would be possible at least to hedge. He took a fresh piece of paper and began to write. Molara paced the room. "What are you writing?" he asked.

"An order to the Commandant of the harbour-forts," replied Miguel promptly, "to acquaint him with the situation and tell him to hold his posts in your name at all hazards."

"It is needless," said Molara; "either his men are traitors or they are not."

"I have told him," said Miguel quickly, "to make a demonstration towards the palace at dawn, if he can trust his men. It will create a diversion."

"Very well," said Molara wearily; "but I doubt it ever reaching him, and he has so few men that could be spared after the forts are held adequately."

An orderly entered with a telegram. The clerk at the office, a loyalist, an unknown man of honour, had brought it himself, passing the line of barricades with extraordinary good-fortune and courage. While the President tore the envelope open, Miguel rose and left the room. Outside in the brilliantly lighted passage he found a servant, terrified but not incapable. He spoke to the man quickly and in a low voice; twenty pounds, the Mayoralty, at all costs, were the essentials of his instructions. Then he re-entered the office.

"Look here," said Molara; "it is not all over yet." The telegram was from Brienz, near Lorenzo: Clear the line. Strelitz and force two thousand rebels advanced on the Black Gorge this afternoon. I have repulsed them with heavy loss. Strelitz is prisoner. Am pursuing remainder. I await instructions at Turga. "This must be published at once," he said. "Get a thousand copies printed, and have them circulated among the loyalists and as far as possible in the city."

The news of the victory was received with cheers by the troops gathered in the palace-square, and they waited with impatience for morning. At length the light of day began to grow in the sky, and other lights, the glow of distant conflagrations, paled. The President, followed by Sorrento, a few officers of high rank, and his aide-de-camp Tiro, descended the steps, traversed the courtyard and passing through the great gates of the palace, entered the square where the last reserves of his power were assembled. He walked about and shook hands right and left with these faithful friends and supporters. Presently his eye caught sight of the rebel proclamation which some daring hand had placed on the wall under cover of the darkness. He walked up and read it by the light of a lantern. Savrola's style was not easy to mistake. The short crisp sentences of the appeal to the people to take up arms rang like a trumpet-call. Across the placard a small red slip, such as are used on theatrical advertisements to show the time of the performance, had been posted at a later hour. It purported to be the facsimile of a telegram and ran thus: Forced Black Gorge this morning. Dictator's troops in full retreat. Am marching on Lorenzo. Strelitz.

Molara quivered with fury. Savrola did not neglect details, and threw few chances away. "Infamous liar!" was the President's comment; but he realised the power of the man he sought to crush, and for a moment despair welled in his heart and seemed to chill his veins. He shook the sensation off with a great effort.

The officers were already in possession of the details of the plan, whose boldness was its main recommendation. The rebels had succeeded in launching their enterprise; the Government would reply by a coup d'état. In any case the stroke was aimed at the heart of the revolt, and if it went home the results would be decisive. "The octopus of Rebellion, Gentlemen," said the President to those around him, and pointing to the Revolutionary proclamation, "has long arms. It will be necessary to cut off his head." And though all felt the venture to be desperate, they were brave men and knew their minds.

The distance from the palace to the Mayoralty was nearly a mile and a half along a broad but winding avenue; by this avenue, and by the narrower streets on either side, the force advanced silently in three divisions. The President marched on foot with the centre column; Sorrento took command of the left, which was the threatened flank. Slowly, and with frequent halts to keep up communication with each other, the troops marched along the silent streets. Not a soul was to be seen: all the shutters of the houses were closed, all the doors fastened; and though the sky grew gradually brighter in the East, the city was still plunged in gloom. The advanced files pressed forward up the avenue, running from tree to tree, and pausing cautiously at each to peer through the darkness. Suddenly as they rounded a bend, a shot rang out in front. "Forward!" cried the President. The bugles sounded the charge and the drums beat. In the dim light the outline of a barricade was visible two hundred yards off, a dark obstruction across the roadway. The soldiers shouted and broke into a run. The defenders of the barricade, surprised, opened an ineffective fire and then, seeing that the attack was in earnest and doubtful of its strength, beat a retreat while time remained. The barricade was captured in a moment, and the assailants pressed on elated by success. Behind the barricade was a cross street, right and left. Firing broke out everywhere, and the loud noise of the rifles echoed from the walls of the houses. The flanking columns had been sharply checked at their barricades, but the capture of the centre position turned both of these, and their defenders, fearing to be cut off, fled in disorder.

It was now daylight, and the scene in the streets was a strange one. The skirmishers darted between the trees, and the little blue-white puffs of smoke spotted the whole picture. The retiring rebels left their wounded on the ground, and these the soldiers bayoneted savagely. Shots were fired from the windows of the houses and from any shelter that offered,—a lamp-post, a pillar-box, a wounded man, an overturned cab. The rifle-fire was searching, and the streets were very bare. In their desire to get cover, to get behind something, both sides broke into the houses and dragged out chairs, tables, and piles of bedding; and though these were but little protection from the bullets, men felt less naked behind them.

All this time the troops were steadily advancing, though suffering continual loss; but gradually the fire of the rebels grew hotter. More men were hurried to the scene each moment; the pressure on the flanks became severe; the enveloping enemy pressed in down the side streets, to hold which the scanty force at the President's disposal had to be further weakened. At length the rebels ceased to retreat; they had reached their guns, four of which were arranged in a row across the avenue.

The Mayoralty was now but a quarter of a mile away, and Molara called on his soldiers for a supreme effort. A dashing attempt to carry the guns with the bayonet was defeated with a loss of thirty killed and wounded, and the Government troops took shelter in a side street at right angles to the main avenue. This in turn was enfiladed by the enemy, who swept round the columns and began to cut in on their line of retreat.

Firing was now general along a wide half-circle. In the hope of driving the improvised artillery-men from their places, the troops forced their way into the houses on either side of the avenue, and climbing along the roofs began to fire down on their adversaries. But the rebels, repeating the manoeuvre, met them and the attempt dwindled into desperate but purposeless fighting among the chimney-pots and the skylights.

The President exposed himself manfully. Moving from one part of the force to another, he animated his followers by his example. Tiro, who kept close to him, had seen enough war to realise that the check was fatal to their chances. Every moment was precious; time was slipping away, and the little force was already almost completely encircled. He had taken a rifle and was assisting to burst in the door of a house, when to his astonishment he saw Miguel. The Secretary was armed. He had hitherto remained

85

carefully in the rear, and had avoided the danger in the air by hiding behind the trees of the avenue; but now he advanced boldly to the doorway and began to help in battering it down. No sooner was this done than he darted in and ran up the stairs crying out, "We are all soldiers to-day!" Several infantrymen followed him to fire from the lowest windows, but Tiro could not leave the President; he felt, however, surprised and pleased by Miguel's gallantry.

It soon became evident to all that the attempt had failed. The numbers against them were too great. A third of the force had been killed or wounded, when the order to cut their way back to the palace was given. On all sides the exulting enemy pressed fiercely. Isolated parties of soldiers, cut off from the retiring column, defended themselves desperately in the houses and on the roofs. They were nearly all killed eventually, for everyone's blood was up, and it was a waste of time to ask for quarter. Others set fire to the houses and tried to escape under cover of the smoke; but very few succeeded. Others again, and among them Miguel, lay hid in closets and cellars, from which they emerged when men's tempers were again human and surrender was not an unknown word. The right column, which consisted of five companies of the Guard battalion, were completely surrounded, and laid down their arms on the promise of a rebel general that their lives should be spared. The promise was kept, and it appeared that the superior officers among the Revolutionists were making great efforts to restrain the fury of their followers.

The main body of the Government troops, massed in a single column, struggled on towards the palace losing men at every step. But in spite of their losses, they were dangerous people to stop. One party of rebels, who intercepted their line of retreat, was swept away in a savage charge, and some attempt was made to reform; but the rifle-fire was pitiless and incessant, and eventually the retreat became a rout. A bloody pursuit followed in which only some eighty men escaped capture or death, and with the President and Sorrento regained the palace alive. The great gates were closed, and the slender garrison prepared to defend themselves to the last.

CHAPTER XVII.

THE DEFENCE OF THE PALACE.

"That," said Lieutenant Tiro to a Captain of Artillery, as they got inside the gate, "is about the best I've seen so far."

"I thought it was a bad business all through," replied the other; "and when they brought the guns up it was a certainty."

"It wasn't the guns that did us," said the Lancer Subaltern, who had no exaggerated idea of the value of artillery; "we wanted some cavalry."

"We wanted more men," answered the Gunner, not anxious at that moment to argue the relative values of the different arms. "These rear-guard actions are the devil."

"There was a damned sight more action than there was rear-guard about that last bit," said Tiro. "Do you suppose they cut up the wounded?"

"Every one of them, I should think; they were like wolves at the end."

"What's going to happen now?"

"They're going to come in here and finish us off."

"We'll see about that," said Tiro. His cheery courage could stand a prolonged test. "The fleet will be back soon; we shall hold this place till then."

The palace was indeed not unsuited to defence. It was solidly built of stone. The windows were at some distance from the ground and the lower strongly barred, except on the garden-side, where the terrace and its steps gave access to the long French windows. But it was evident that a few good rifles could forbid the bare and narrow approaches in that quarter. Indeed it seemed as though the architect must have contemplated the occasion that had now arrived, for he had almost built a stronghold disguised as a palace. The side which faced the square seemed to afford the best prospects to an assault; yet the great gate was protected by two small towers containing guard-rooms, and the wall of the courtyard was high and thick. As it seemed, however, that on this front the enemy would be able to use their numbers to the greatest effect, the majority of the little garrison were concentrated there.

The rebels were wisely and cautiously led. They did not at once push on to the attack of the palace; sure of their prey they could afford to wait. Meanwhile the surviving adherents of the Government endeavoured to make their last foothold secure. Rough-hewn cobblestones from the pavements of the courtyard were prized up, and the windows were with these converted into loopholes through which the garrison might fire without much exposure. The gates were closed and barred, and preparations made to strut them with baulks of timber. Ammunition was distributed. The duty and responsibility of each section of the defence was apportioned to the various officers. The defenders recognised that they had entered on a quarrel which must be carried to a definite conclusion.

But Molara's mood had changed. The fury of the night had cooled into the hard, savage courage of the morning. He had led the desperate attempt to capture the Mayoralty, and had exposed himself freely and even recklessly in the tumult of the fight that followed; but now that he had come through unhurt, had regained the palace, and realised that his last chance of killing Savrola had passed, death appeared very ugly. All the excitement which had supported him had died away; he had had enough. His mind searched for some way of escape, and searched vainly. The torture of the moment was keen. A few hours might bring help: the fleet would surely come; but it would be too late. The great guns might take vengeance for his death; they could not save his life. A feeling of vexation shook him, and behind it grew the realisation of the approaching darkness. Terror began to touch his heart; his nerve flickered; he had more to fear than the others.

The hatred of the multitude was centred in him; after all it was his blood they wanted,—his above all others. It was a dreadful distinction. He retired in deep despondency to his own room, and took no part in the defence.

At about eleven o'clock the sharpshooters of the enemy began to make their way into the houses which surrounded the front of the palace. Presently from an upper window a shot was fired; others followed, and soon a regular fusilade began. The defenders, sheltered by their walls, replied carefully. Lieutenant Tiro and a sergeant of the Guards, an old war-time comrade of Molara's, were holding the window of the guard-room on the left of the great gate. Both were good shots. The Subaltern had filled his pockets with cartridges; the Sergeant arranged his on the sill in neat little rows of five. From their position they could shoot right down the street which led into the square and towards the gate. Outside the guard-room a dozen officers and men were still engaged in making the entrance more secure. They tried to wedge a great plank between the ground and the second cross-piece; should the rebels try to rush the gate-way, it would thus be strong enough to resist them.

The fire from the surrounding houses was annoying rather than dangerous, but several bullets struck the stones of the improvised loopholes. The garrison fired carefully and slowly, anxious not to expend their ammunition, or to expose themselves without a result. Suddenly, about three hundred yards away, a number of men turned into the street which led to the gate, and began rapidly pushing and pulling something forward.

"Look out," cried Tiro to the working-party; "they're bringing up a gun;" and taking good aim he fired at the approaching enemy. The Sergeant, and all the other defenders of this side of the palace, fired too with strange energy. The advancing crowd slackened speed. Among them men began to drop. Several in front threw up their hands; others began carrying these away. The attack dwindled. Then two or three men ran back alone. At that all the rest turned tail and scurried for the cover of the side street, leaving the gun (one of the captured twelve-pounders) standing deserted in the middle of the roadway, with about a dozen shapeless black objects lying round it.

The garrison raised a cheer, which was answered from the surrounding houses by an increase of musketry.

A quarter of an hour passed and then the rebels debouched from the side streets into the main approach and began pushing up four carts filled with sacks of flour. Again the defenders fired rapidly. Their bullets, striking the sacks, raised strange creamy white clouds; but the assailants, sheltered by their movable cover, continued to advance steadily. They reached the gun, and began emptying the carts by pushing the sacks out from behind, until a regular breastwork was formed, behind which they knelt down. Some began firing; others devoted their efforts to discharging the gun, on which the aim of the garrison was now directed. With a loss of two men they succeeded in loading it and pointing it at the gate. A third man advanced to fix the friction-tube by which it was fired.

Tiro took steady aim and the distant figure collapsed to the shot.

"Bull's eye," said the Sergeant appreciatively, and leaned forward to fire at another, who had advanced with desperate bravery to discharge the piece. He paused long on his aim, wishing to make certain; holding his breath he began gently to squeeze the trigger, as the musketry-books enjoin. Suddenly there was a very strange sound, half thud, half smash. Tiro, shrinking swiftly to the left, just avoided being splashed with blood and other physical details. The Sergeant had been killed by a bullet which had come to meet him as he looked through his loophole. The distant man had fixed his tube, and, catching up the lanyard, stood back and aside to fire.

"Stand from the gate," shouted Tiro to the working-party; "I can't hold 'em!" He raised his rifle and fired on the chance. At the same instant a great cloud of smoke burst from the gun and another sprang up at the palace gate. The woodwork was smashed to pieces and, with the splinters of the shell, flew on, overtaking with death and wounds the working-party as they scampered to cover.

A long loud burst of cheering arose on all sides from the surrounding houses and streets, and was taken up by the thousands who were waiting behind and heard the explosion of the gun. At first the rebel fire increased, but very soon a bugler began to sound perseveringly, and after about twenty minutes the musketry ceased altogether. Then from over the barricade a man with a white flag advanced, followed by two others. The truce was acknowledged from the palace by the waving of a handkerchief. The deputation walked straight up to the shattered gateway, and their leader, stepping through, entered the courtyard. Many of the defenders left their stations to look at him and hear what terms were offered. It was Moret.

"I call upon you all to surrender," he said. "Your lives will be spared until you have been fairly tried."

"Address yourself to me, Sir," said Sorrento stepping forward; "I am in command here."

"I call upon you all to surrender in the name of the Republic," repeated Moret loudly.

"I forbid you to address these soldiers," said Sorrento. "If you do so again, your flag shall not protect you."

Moret turned to him. "Resistance is useless," he said. "Why will you cause further loss of life? Surrender, and your lives shall be safe."

Sorrento reflected. Perhaps the rebels knew that the fleet was approaching; otherwise, he thought they would not offer terms. It was necessary to gain time. "We shall require two hours fro consider the terms," he said.

"No," answered Moret decidedly. "You must surrender at once, here and now."

"We shall do no such thing," replied the War-Minister. "The palace is defensible. We shall hold it until the return of the fleet and of the victorious field-army."

"You refuse all terms?"

"We refuse all you have offered."

"Soldiers," said Moret turning again to the men, "I implore you not to throw away your lives. I offer fair terms; do not reject them."

"Young man," said Sorrento with rising anger, "I have a somewhat lengthy score to settle with you already. You are a civilian and are ignorant of the customs of war. It is my duty to warn you that, if you continue to attempt to seduce the loyalty of the Government troops, I shall fire at you." He drew his revolver.

Moret should have heeded; but tactless, brave, and impulsive as he was, he recked little. His warm heart generously hoped to save further loss of life. Besides, he did not believe that Sorrento would shoot him in cold blood; it would be too merciless. "I offer you all life," he cried; "do not choose death."

Sorrento raised his pistol and fired. Moret fell to the ground, and his blood began to trickle over the white flag. For a moment he twisted and quivered, and then lay still. There were horrified murmurs from the bystanders, who had not expected to see the threat carried out. But it is not well to count on the mercy of such men as this War-Minister; they live their lives too much by rule and regulation.

The two men outside the gate, hearing the shot, looked in, saw, and ran swiftly back to their comrades, while the garrison, feeling that they must now abandon all hope, returned to their posts slowly and sullenly. The report of a truce had drawn the President from his room, with a fresh prospect of life, and perhaps of vengeance, opening on his imagination. As he came down the steps into the courtyard, the shot, in such close proximity, startled him; when he saw the condition of the bearer of terms, he staggered. "Good God!" he said to Sorrento, "what have you done?"

"I have shot a rebel, Sir," replied the War-Minister, his heart full of misgivings, but trying to brazen it out, "for inciting the troops to mutiny and desertion, after due warning that his flag would no longer protect him."

Molara quivered from head to foot; he felt the last retreat cut off. "You have condemned us all to death," he said. Then he stooped and drew a paper which protruded from the dead man's coat. It ran as follows: I authorise you to accept the surrender of Antonio Molara, ex-President of the Republic, and of such officers, soldiers, and adherents as may be holding the Presidential Palace. Their lives are to be spared, and they shall be protected pending the decision of the Government. For the Council of Public Safety,—SAVROLA. And Sorrento had killed him,—the only man who could save them from the fury of the crowd. Too sick at heart to speak Molara turned away, and as he did so the firing from the houses of the square recommenced with savage vigour. The besiegers knew now how their messenger had fared.

And all the while Moret lay very still out there in the courtyard. All his ambitions, his enthusiasms, his hopes had come to a full stop; his share in the world's affairs was over; he had sunk into the ocean of the past, and left scarcely a bubble behind. In all the contriving of the plot against the Lauranian Government Savrola's personality had dwarfed his. Yet this was a man of heart and brain and nerve, one who might have

90

accomplished much; and he had a mother and two young sisters who loved the soil he trod on, and thought him the finest fellow in the world.

Sorrento stood viewing his handiwork for a long time, with a growing sense of dissatisfaction at his deed. His sour, hard nature was incapable of genuine remorse, but he had known Molara for many years and was shocked to see his pain, and annoyed to think that he was the cause. He had not realised that the President wished to surrender; otherwise, he said to himself, he might have been more lenient. Was there no possible way of repairing the harm? The man who had authorised Moret to accept their surrender had power with the crowd; he would be at the Mayoralty,—he must be sent for,—but how?

Lieutenant Tiro approached with a coat in his hands. Disgusted at his superior's brutality, he was determined to express his feelings, clearly if not verbally. He bent over the body and composed the limbs; then he laid the coat over the white expressionless face, and rising said insolently to the Colonel: "I wonder if they'll do that for you in a couple of hours' time, Sir."

Sorrento looked at him, and laughed harshly. "Pooh! What do I care? When you have seen as much fighting as I have, you will not be so squeamish."

"I am not likely to see much more, now that you have killed the only man who could accept our surrender."

"There is another," said the War-Minister, "Savrola. If you want to live, go and bring him to call off his hounds."

Sorrento spoke bitterly, but his words set the Subaltern's mind working. Savrola,— he knew him, liked him, and felt they had something in common. Such a one would come if he were summoned; but to leave the palace seemed impossible. Although the attacks of the rebels had been directed against the side of the main entrance only, a close investment and a dropping musketry were maintained throughout the complete circle. To pass the line of besiegers by the roads was out of the question. Tiro thought of the remaining alternatives: a tunnel, that did not exist; a balloon, there was not one. Shaking his head at the hopeless problem he gazed contemplatively into the clear air, thinking to himself: "It would take a bird to do it."

The palace was connected with the Senate-House and with the principal Public Offices by telephone, and it happened that the main line of wires from the eastern end of the great city passed across its roof. Tiro, looking up, saw the slender threads overhead; there seemed to be nearly twenty of them. The War-Minister followed his gaze. "Could you get along the wires?" he asked eagerly.

"I will try," answered the Subaltern, thrilled with the idea.

Sorrento would have shaken his hand, but the boy stepped backward and saluting turned away. He entered the palace, and ascended the stairs which led to the flat roof. The attempt was daring and dangerous. What if the rebels should see him in mid air? He had often shot with a pea-rifle at rooks, black spots against the sky and among the branches.

91

The thought seemed strangely disagreeable; but he consoled himself with the reflection that men who look through loopholes at the peril of their lives have little leisure for aught but aiming, and rarely let their eyes wander idly. He stepped out on to the roof and walked to the telegraph-post. There was no doubt as to its strength; nevertheless he paused, for the chances against him were great, and death seemed near and terrible. His religion, like that of many soldiers, was of little help; it was merely a jumble of formulas, seldom repeated, hardly understood, never investigated, and a hopeful, but unauthorised, belief that it would be well with him if he did his duty like a gentleman. He had no philosophy; he felt only that he was risking all that he had, and for what he was uncertain. Still, though there were gaps in his reasoning, he thought it might be done and he would have a dash for it. He said to himself, "It will score off those swine," and with this inspiring reflection he dismissed his fears.

He swarmed up the pole to the lowest wire; then he pulled himself higher until he could get his foot on the insulators. The wires ran on both sides of the pole in two sets. He stood on the two lowest, took the top ones under his arms, and, reaching down over, caught one more in each hand. Then he started, shuffling awkwardly along. The span was about seventy yards. As he cleared the parapet he saw the street beneath him,—very far beneath him, it seemed. Shots were continually exchanged from the windows of the houses and the palace. Sixty feet below a dead man lay staring up through the wires undazzled by the bright sun. He had been under fire before, but this was a novel experience. As he approached the middle of the span the wires began to swing, and he had to hold on tightly. At first the slope had been on his side, but after the centre was passed it rose against him; his feet slipped often backwards, and the wires commenced to cut into his armpits.

Two-thirds of the distance was safely accomplished, when the wires under his left foot parted with a snap and dropped like a whip-lash against the wall of the opposite house. His weight fell on his shoulders; the pain was sharp; he twisted,—slipped,— clutched wildly, and recovered himself by a tremendous effort.

A man at a lower window pulled back the mattress behind which he was firing and thrust his head and shoulders out. Tiro looked down and their eyes met. The man shouted in mad excitement, and fired his rifle point-blank at the Subaltern. The noise of the report prevented him from knowing how near the bullet had passed; but he felt he was not shot, and struggled on till he had passed the street.

It was all up; yet to turn back was equally fatal. "I'll see it out," he said to himself, and dropped from the wires on to the roof of the house. The door from the leads was open. Running down the attic stairs and emerging on the landing, he peered over the bannisters; no one was to be seen. He descended the narrow staircase cautiously, wondering where his enemy could be. Presently he was opposite the front room on the second floor. Keeping close to the wall he peered in. The room was half-darkened. The windows were blocked by boxes, portmanteaus, mattresses, and pillow-cases filled with earth; broken glass, mingled with bits of plaster from the walls, littered the floor. By the light which filtered in through the chinks and loopholes, he saw a strange scene. There were four men in the room; one on his back on the ground, and the others bending over him. Their rifles were leaned against the wall. They seemed to have eyes only for their comrade who lay on the floor in an ever-widening pool of blood, gurgling, choking, and apparently making tremendous efforts to speak.

The Subaltern had seen enough. Opposite the front room was a doorway covered by a curtain, behind which he glided. Nothing was to be seen, but he listened intently.

"Poor chap," said a voice, "he's got it real bad."

"How did it happen?" asked another.

"Oh, he leaned out of the window to have a shot,—bullet hit him,—right through the lungs, I think,—fired in the air, and shouted." Then in a lower but still audible tone he added, "Done for!"

The wounded man began making extraordinary noises.

"Su'thin' he wants to tell 'is pore wife before he goes," said one of the Revolutionaries, who seemed by his speech a workman. "What is it, mate?"

"Give him a pencil and paper; he can't speak."

Tiro's heart stood still, and his hand stole back for his revolver.

For nearly a minute nothing audible happened; then there was a shout.

"By God, we'll cop him!" said the workman, and all three of them stamped past the curtained door and ran up-stairs. One man paused just opposite; he was loading his rifle and the cartridge stuck; he banged it on the ground, apparently with success, for the Subaltern heard the bolt click, and the swift footsteps followed the others towards the roof.

Then he emerged from his hiding-place and stole downwards. But as he passed the open room he could not resist looking in. The wounded man saw him in an instant. He half raised himself from the ground and made terrible efforts to shout; but no articulate sound came forth. Tiro looked for a moment at this stranger whom chance had made his implacable enemy, and then, at the prompting of that cruel devil that lurks in the hearts of men and is awakened by bloodshed and danger, he kissed his hand to him in savage, bitter mockery. The other sank backwards in a paroxysm of pain and fury and lay gasping on the floor. The Subaltern hurried away. Reaching the lowest storey he turned into the kitchen, where the window was but six feet from the ground. Vaulting on to the sill he dropped into the backyard, and then, with a sudden feeling of wild panic, began to run at top speed,—the terror that springs from returning hope hard on his track.

CHAPTER XVIII.

# FROM A WINDOW.

While the swift succession of great events in the Lauranian capital had occupied with immediate emergency the minds of the men, it had been different with the women. Out in the streets there had been vivid scenes, hot blood, and excitement. The dangers of war, and the occasion of close and involved fighting, had given many opportunities for acts of devotion and brutality. The brave man had displayed his courage; the cruel had indulged his savagery; all the intermediate types had been thrilled with the business of the moment, and there had scarce been time for any but involuntary terror. Within the houses it was different.

Lucile started up at the first sound of firing. There was not much to hear, a distant and confused popping with an occasional ragged crash; but she knew what all this meant and shuddered. The street below seemed from the noise to be full of people. She rose and going to the window looked down. By the sickly, uncertain light of the gas-lamps men were working busily at a barricade, which ran across the street about twenty yards from the door and on the side towards the palace. She watched the bustling figures with strange interest. They distracted her thoughts and she felt that if she had nothing to look at she would go mad with the dreadful suspense. Not a detail escaped her.

How hard they worked! Men with crowbars and pickaxes were prizing up the paving-stones; others carried them along, staggering under their weight; others again piled them into a strong wall across the road. There were two or three boys working away as hard as any of them. One little fellow dropped the stone he was carrying on his foot, and forthwith sat down to cry bitterly. His companion came up and kicked him to stimulate his efforts, but he only cried the more. Presently a water-cart arrived, and the thirsty builders went by threes and fours to drink, dipping two tin mugs and a gallipot in the water.

The people in the houses round were made to open their doors, and the rebels unceremoniously dragged out all sorts of things to put on their barricade. One party discovered several barrels which they appeared to consider a valuable prize. Knocking in the end of one cask they began filling it, spadeful by spadeful, with the earth which the removal of the pavement had laid bare. It was a long business, but at last they finished and tried to lift the barrel on to the wall; but it was too heavy, and falling with a crash to the ground it broke all in pieces. At this they were furious and disputed angrily, till an officer with a red sash came up and silenced them. They did not attempt to fill the other casks, but re-entering the house brought out a comfortable sofa and sat down on it sullenly, lighting their pipes. One by one, however, they got to work again, coming out of their sulky fit by degrees, and careful of their dignity. And all this time the barricade grew steadily.

Lucile wondered why no one had entered Savrola's house. Presently she perceived the reason; there was a picket of four men with rifles on the doorstep. Nothing had been forgotten by that comprehensive mind. So the hours passed. From time to time her thoughts reverted to the tragedy which had swept upon her life, and she would sink back on to the sofa in despair. Once, from sheer weariness, she dozed for an hour. The distant firing had died away and, though single shots were occasionally heard, the city was

94

generally silent. Waking with a strange feeling of uneasy trouble she ran again to the window. The barricade was completed now, and the builders were lying down behind it. Their weapons leaned against the wall on which two or three watchers stood, looking constantly up the street.

Presently there was a hammering at the street-door, which made her heart beat with fear. She leaned cautiously out of the window. The picket was still at its post, but another man had joined them. Finding that he could not obtain an answer to his knocking, he stooped down, pushed something under the door, and went his way. After a time she summoned up courage to creep down, through the darkness of the staircase, to see what this might be. By the light of a match she saw that it was a note addressed simply Lucile with the number of the house and street,—for the streets were all numbered in Laurania as in American cities. It was from Savrola, in pencil and to this effect: The city and forts have passed into our hands, but there will be fighting at daylight. On no account leave the house or expose yourself.

Fighting at daylight! She looked at the clock,—a quarter to five, and already the sky was growing brighter; the time was at hand then! Fear, grief, anxiety, and, not the least painful, resentment at her husband conflicted in her mind. But the sleeping figures behind the barricade seemed to be troubled by none of these feelings; they lay silent and still, weary men who had no cares. But she knew it was coming, something loud and terrible that would wake them with a start. She felt as though she was watching a play at the theatre, the window suggesting a box. She had turned from it for a moment, when suddenly a rifle-shot rang out, apparently about three hundred yards down the street towards the palace. Then there was a splutter of firing, a bugle-call, and the sound of shouting. The defenders of the barricade sprang up in mad haste and seized their weapons. There was more firing, but still they did not reply, and she dared not put her head out of the window to see what prevented them. They were all greatly excited, holding their rifles over the barricade, and many talking in quick short sentences. In a moment a crowd of men, nearly a hundred it seemed, ran up to the wall and began scrambling over, helped by the others. They were friends, then; it occurred to her that there must be another barricade, and that the one under the window was in the second line. This was actually the case, and the first had been captured. All the time firing from the direction of the palace continued.

As soon as the fugitives were all across the wall, the defenders of the second line began to fire. The rifles close by sounded so much louder than the others, and gave forth such bright flashes. But the light was growing every minute, and soon she could see the darting puffs of smoke. The rebels were armed with many kinds of firearms. Some, with old, muzzle-loading muskets, had to stand up and descend from the barricade to use their ramrods; others, armed with more modern weapons, remained crouching behind their cover and fired continually.

The scene, filled with little foreshortened figures, still suggested the stage of a theatre viewed from the gallery. She did not as yet feel frightened; no harm had been done, and no one seemed to be any the worse.

She had scarcely completed this thought when she noticed a figure being lifted off the barricade to the ground. In the growing daylight the pale face showed distinctly, and a deadly feeling of sickness came over her in a moment; but she stood spell-bound by the sight. Four men went off with the wounded one, carrying him by the shoulders and feet, so that he drooped in the middle. When they had passed out of her view, she looked back to the wall. There were five more men wounded; four had to be carried, the other leaned on a comrade's arm. Two more figures had also been pulled off the barricade, and laid carelessly on the pavement out of the way. Nobody seemed to take any notice of these, but just let them lie close to the area-railings.

Then from the far end of the street came the sound of drums and the shrill call of a bugle, repeated again and again. The rebels began to shoot in mad excitement as fast as they could; several fell, and above the noise of the firing rose a strange sound, a sort of hoarse, screaming whoop, coming momentarily nearer.

A man on the barricade jumped off and began to run down the street; five, six others followed at once; then all the defenders but three hurried away from that strange approaching cry. Several tried to drag with them the wounded, of which there already were a few more; these cried out in pain and begged to be left alone. One man, she saw, dragging another by the ankle, bumping him along the rough roadway in spite of his entreaties. The three men who had stayed fired methodically from behind their breastwork. All this took several seconds; and the menacing shout came nearer and louder all the time.

Then in an instant a wave of men,—soldiers in blue uniforms faced with buff— surged up to the barricade and over it. An officer, quite a boy, in front of them all, jumped down the other side, shouting, "Make a clear sweep of the cowardly devils,— come on!"

The three steadfast men had disappeared as rocks beneath the incoming tide. Crowds of soldiers climbed over the barricade; she could see groups of them swarming round each of the wounded rebels, jobbing downwards with their bayonets savagely. And then the spell broke, the picture swam, and she rushed screaming from the window to plunge her face among the sofa-cushions.

The uproar was now terrific. The musketry-fire was loud and continuous, especially from the direction of the main avenue which ran parallel to the street in which Savrola lived, and the shouting and trampling of men added to the din. Gradually the wave of fighting rolled past the house and on towards the Mayoralty. As she realised this, all her own troubles returned to her mind. The fight was going against the rebels; she thought of Savrola. And then she prayed,—prayed convulsively, sending her entreaties into space in the hope that they would not fall on unheeding ears. She spoke no name; but the gods, who are omniscient, may have guessed, with sardonic smiles, that she prayed for the victory of the rebel she loved over her husband, the President.

Presently there was a tremendous noise from the direction of the Mayoralty. "Cannons," she thought, but she dared not look out of the window; the horrid sights had sickened curiosity itself. But she could hear the fire coming nearer, coming back again; and at that she felt a strange joy; something of the joy of success in war, amid all her terrors. There was a noise of people streaming past the house; shots were fired under the windows; then came a great hammering and battering at the street-door. They were breaking into the house! She rushed to the door of the room and locked it. Down-stairs there were several shots, and the noise of splintering wood. The firing of the retreating troops drifted back past the house and towards the palace; but she did not heed it; another sound paralysed her attention, the sound of approaching footsteps. Someone was coming up-stairs. She held her breath. The handle turned, and then the unknown, finding the door locked, kicked it savagely. Lucile screamed.

The kicking ceased, and she heard the stranger give a dreadful groan. "For the mercy of Heaven, let me in! I am wounded and have no arms." He began to wail pitifully.

Lucile listened. It seemed that there was but one, and if he were wounded, he would not harm her. There was another groan outside. Human sympathy rose in her heart; she unlocked the door and opened it cautiously.

A man walked quickly into the room: it was Miguel. "I beg Your Excellency's pardon," he said suavely, with that composure which always strengthened his mean soul; "I am in need of a hiding-place."

"But your wound?" she said.

"A ruse-de-guerre; I wanted you to let me in. Where can I hide? They may be here soon."

"There on the roof, or in the observatory," she said pointing to the other door.

"Do not tell them."

"Why should I?" she replied. Calm though the man undoubtedly was, she despised him; there was no dirt, she knew well, that he would not eat if it suited his purpose to do so.

He went up and concealed himself on the roof under the big telescope. Meanwhile she waited. Emotions had succeeded each other so rapidly that day in her heart that she felt incapable of further stress; a dull feeling of pain remained, like the numbness and sense of injury after a severe wound. The firing receded towards the palace, and presently all was comparatively silent in the city again.

At about nine o'clock the bell of the front-entrance rang; but she did not dare to leave the room now that the door was broken down. Then after a while came the sound of people coming up-stairs.

"There is no lady here; the young lady went back the night before last to her aunt's," said a voice. It was the old woman's; with a bound of joy and a passionate craving for the sympathy of her own sex, Lucile rushed to the door and opened it. Bettine was there, and with her an officer of the rebel army, who handed a letter to her with these words: "The President sends this to you, Madam."

"The President!"

"Of the Council of Public Safety."

The note merely informed her that the Government troops had been repulsed and ended with the words: Only one result is now possible, and that will be attained in a few hours.

The officer, saying that he would wait down-stairs in case she might wish to send an answer, left the room. Lucile pulled the old nurse inside the door and embraced her, weeping. Where had she been all that terrible night? Bettine had been in the cellar. It seemed that Savrola had thought of her as of everything; he had told her to take her bed down there, and had even had the place carpeted and furnished on the preceding afternoon. There she had remained as he had told her. Her perfect trust in her idol had banished all fears on her own account, but she had "fidgeted terribly" about him. He was all she had in the world; others dissipate their affections on a husband, children, brothers, and sisters; all the love of her kind old heart was centred in the man she had fostered since he was a helpless baby. And he did not forget. She displayed with pride a slip of paper, bearing the words, Safe and well.

There was now a subdued sound of firing, from the direction of the palace, which continued throughout the morning; but Miguel, seeing that the streets were again quiet, emerged from his concealment and re-entered the room. "I want to see the President," he said.

"My husband?" asked Lucile.

"No, Your Excellency, Señor Savrola." Miguel was quick in adapting himself to circumstances.

Lucile thought of the officer; she mentioned him to Miguel. "He will take you to the Mayoralty."

The Secretary was delighted; he ran down-stairs and they saw him no more.

The old nurse, with a practical soul, busied herself about getting breakfast. Lucile, to divert her thoughts, aided her, and soon—such is our composition—found comfort in eggs and bacon. They were relieved to find that a picket had again been posted at the street-door. Bettine discovered this, for Lucile, her mood unchanged, would not look into the street where she had seen such grim spectacles. And she did right, for though the barricade was now deserted, nearly twenty objects that had a few hours before been men, lay around or upon it. But about eleven some labourers arrived with two scavengers' carts; and soon only the bloodstains on the pavement showed that there had been any destruction other than that of property.

The morning wore slowly and anxiously away. The firing near the palace was continual, but distant. Sometimes it swelled into a dull roar, at others the individual shots sounded in a sort of quick rattle. At last, at about half-past two, it stopped abruptly. Lucile trembled. The quarrel had been decided, one way or the other. Her mind refused to face all the possibilities. At times she clung in passionate fear to the old nurse, who tried in vain to soothe her; at others she joined her in the household tasks, or submitted to tasting the various meals which the poor old soul prepared for her in the hopes of killing care with comfort.

The ominous silence that followed the cessation of the firing did not last long. It was while Lucile was being coaxed by Bettine to eat some custard-pudding that she had made on purpose for her, that the report of the first great gun reached them. The tremendous explosion, though a long way off, made the windows rattle. She shuddered. What was this? She had hoped that all was over; but one explosion succeeded another, until the thunder of a cannonade from the harbour almost drowned their voices. It was a weary waiting for the two women.

CHAPTER XIX.

AN EDUCATIONAL EXPERIENCE.

Lieutenant Tiro reached the Mayoralty in safety, for though the streets were full of excited people, they were peaceful citizens, and on his proclaiming that he had been sent to see Savrola they allowed him to pass. The Municipal building was a magnificent structure of white stone, elaborately decorated with statuary and sculpture. In front of it, surrounded by iron railings and accessible by three gateways, stretched a wide courtyard, in which a great fountain, encircled by the marble figures of departed civic magnates, played continually with agreeable effect. The whole edifice was worthy of the riches and splendour of the Lauranian capital.

Two sentries of the rebel forces stood on guard with fixed bayonets at the central gateway, and allowed none to enter without due authority. Messengers were hurrying across the courtyard incessantly, and orderlies coming or going at a gallop. Without the gates a large crowd, for the most part quiet, though greatly agitated, filled the broad thoroughfare. Wild rumours circulated at random in the mass and the excitement was intense. The sound of distant firing was distinct and continuous.

Tiro made his way through the crowd without much difficulty, but found his path blocked by the sentries at the gateway. They refused to allow him to proceed, and for a moment he feared that he had run his risks in vain. Luckily, however, he was recognised as Molara's aide-de-camp by one of the Municipal attendants who were loitering in the courtyard. He wrote his name on a piece of paper and requested the man to take it to Savrola or, as he was now styled, the President of the Council of Public Safety. The servant departed, and after ten minutes returned with an officer, resplendent with the red sash of the Revolutionary party, who bade the Subaltern follow him forthwith.

The hall of the Mayoralty was full of excited and voluble patriots who were eager to serve the cause of Liberty, if it could be done without risking their lives. They all wore red sashes and talked loudly, discussing the despatches from the fight which arrived by frequent messengers and were posted on the walls. Tiro and his guide passed through the hall and hurrying along a passage arrived at the entrance of a small committee-room. Several ushers and messengers stood around it; an officer was on duty outside. He opened the door and announced the Subaltern.

"Certainly," said a well-known voice, and Tiro entered. It was a small, wainscotted apartment with two tall and deeply set glazed windows shaded by heavy, faded curtains of reddish hue. Savrola was writing at a table in the middle of the room; Godoy and Renos were talking near one of the windows; another man, whom for the moment he did not recognise, was busily scribbling in the corner. The great Democrat looked up.

"Good-morning, Tiro," he said cheerily, then, seeing the serious and impatient look on the boy's face, he asked him what had happened. Tiro told him quickly of the President's wish to surrender the palace. "Well," said Savrola, "Moret is there, and he has full powers."

"He is dead."

"How?" asked Savrola, in a low pained voice.

"Shot in the throat," replied the Subaltern laconically.

Savrola had turned very white; he was fond of Moret and they had long been friends. A feeling of disgust at the whole struggle came over him; he repressed it; this was no time for regrets. "You mean that the crowd will accept no surrender?"

"I mean they have probably massacred them all by now."

"What time was Moret killed?"

"A quarter-past twelve."

Savrola took up a paper that lay beside him on the table. "This was sent off at half-past twelve."

Tiro looked at it. It was signed Moret and ran as follows: Am preparing for final assault. All well.

"It is a forgery," said the Subaltern simply. "I started myself before the half-hour, and Señor Moret had been dead ten minutes then. Somebody has assumed the command."

"By Jove," said Savrola getting up from the table. "Kreutze!" He caught up his hat and cane. "Come on; he will most certainly murder Molara, and probably the others, if he is not stopped. I must go there myself."

"What?" said Renos. "Most irregular; your place is here."

"Send an officer," suggested Godoy.

"I have none to send of sufficient power with the people, unless you will go yourself."

"I! No, certainly not! I would not think of it," said Godoy quickly. "It would be useless; I have no authority over the mob."

"That is not quite the tone you have adopted all the morning," replied Savrola quietly, "or at least since the Government attack was repulsed." Then turning to Tiro, he said, "Let us start."

They were leaving the room when the Subaltern saw that the man who had been writing in the corner was looking at him. To his astonishment he recognised Miguel.

The Secretary bowed satirically. "Here we are again," he said; "you were wise to follow."

"You insult me," said Tiro with profound contempt. "Rats leave a sinking ship."

"The wiser they," rejoined the Secretary; "they could do no good by staying. I have always heard that aides-de-camp are the first to leave a fight."

"You are a damned dirty dog," said the Subaltern falling back on a rudimentary form of repartee with which he was more familiar.

"I can wait no longer," said Savrola in a voice that was a plain command. Tiro obeyed, and they left the room.

Walking down the passage and through the hall, where Savrola was loudly cheered, they reached the entrance, where a carriage was waiting. A dozen mounted men, with red sashes and rifles, ranged themselves about it as an escort. The crowd outside the gates, seeing the great leader and hearing the applause within, raised a shout. Savrola turned to the commander of the escort. "I need no guard," he said; "that is necessary only for tyrants. I will go alone." The escort fell back. The two men entered the carriage and, drawn by strong horses, passed out into the streets.

"You dislike Miguel?" asked Savrola after a while.

"He is a traitor."

"There are plenty about the city. Now I suppose you would call me a traitor."

"Ah! but you have always been one," replied Tiro bluntly. Savrola gave a short laugh. "I mean," continued the other, "that you have always been trying to upset things."

"I have been loyal to my treachery," suggested Savrola.

"Yes,—we have always been at war with you; but this viper——"

101

"Well," said Savrola, "you must take men as you find them; few are disinterested. The viper, as you call him, is a poor creature; but he saved my life, and asked me to save his in return. What could I do? Besides he is of use. He knows the exact state of the public finances and is acquainted with the details of the foreign policy. What are we stopping for?"

Tiro looked out. The street was closed by a barricade which made it a cul-de-sac. "Try the next turning," he said to the coachman; "go on quickly." The noise of the firing could now be distinctly heard. "We very nearly pulled it off this morning," said Tiro.

"Yes," answered Savrola; "they told me the attack was repulsed with difficulty."

"Where were you?" asked the boy in great astonishment.

"At the Mayoralty, asleep; I was very tired."

Tiro was conscious of an irresistible feeling of disgust. So he was a coward, this great man. He had always heard that politicians took care of their skins, and sent others to fight their battles. Somehow he had thought that Savrola was different: he knew such a lot about polo; but he was the same as all the rest.

Savrola, ever quick to notice, saw his look and again laughed dryly. "You think I ought to have been in the streets? Believe me, I did more good where I was. If you had seen the panic and terror at the Mayoralty during the fighting, you would have recognised that there were worse things to do than to go to sleep in confidence. Besides, everything in human power had been done; and we had not miscalculated."

Tiro remained unconvinced. His good opinion of Savrola was destroyed. He had heard much of this man's political courage. The physical always outweighed the moral in his mind. He felt reluctantly convinced that he was a mere word-spinner, brave enough where speeches were concerned, but careful when sterner work was to be done.

The carriage stopped again. "All these streets are barricaded, Sir," said the coach-man.

Savrola looked out of the window. "We are close there, let us walk; it is only half a mile across Constitution Square." He jumped out. The barricade was deserted, as were the streets in this part of the town. Most of the violent rebels were attacking the palace, and the peaceable citizens were in their houses or outside the Mayoralty.

They scrambled over the rough wail, which was made of paving-stones and sacks of earth piled under and upon two waggons, and hurried down the street beyond. It led to the great square of the city. At the further end was the Parliament House, with the red flag of revolt flying from its tower. An entrenchment had been dug in front of the entrance, and the figures of some of the rebel soldiery were visible on it.

They had gone about a quarter of the distance across the square, when suddenly, from the entrenchment or barricade three hundred yards away, there darted a puff of smoke; five or six more followed in quick succession. Savrola paused, astonished, but the

102

Subaltern understood at once. "Run for it!" he cried. "The statue,—there is cover behind it."

Savrola began to run as fast as he could. The firing from the barricade continued. He heard two sucking kisses in the air; something struck the pavement in front of him so that the splinters flew, and while he passed a grey smudge appeared; there was a loud tang on the area-railings beside him; the dust of the roadway sprang up in several strange spurts. As he ran, the realisation of what these things meant grew stronger; but the distance was short and he reached the statue alive. Behind its massive pedestal there was ample shelter for both.

"They fired at us."

"They did," replied Tiro. "Damn them!"

"But why?"

"My uniform—devilry—running man—good fun, you know—for them."

"We must go on," said Savrola.

"We can't go on across the square."

"Which way, then?"

"We must work down the street away from them, keeping the statue between us and their fire, and get up one of the streets to the left."

A main street ran through the centre of the great square, and led out of it at right angles to the direction in which they were proceeding. It was possible to retire down this under cover of the statue, and to take a parallel street further along. This would enable them to avoid the fire from the entrenchment, or would at least reduce the dangerous space to a few yards. Savrola looked in the direction Tiro indicated. "Surely this is shorter," he said pointing across the square.

"Much shorter," answered the Subaltern; "in about three seconds it will take you to another world."

Savrola rose. "Come on," he said; "I do not allow such considerations to affect my judgment. The lives of men are at stake; the time is short. Besides, this is an educational experience."

The blood was in his cheeks and his eyes sparkled; all that was reckless in him, all his love of excitement, stirred in his veins. Tiro looked at him amazed. Brave as he was, he saw no pleasure in rushing to his death at the heels of a mad politician; but he allowed no man to show him the way. He said no more, but drew back to the far end of the pedestal, so as to gain pace, and then bounded into the open and ran as fast as he could run.

103

How he got across he never knew. One bullet cut the peak of his cap, another tore his trousers. He had seen many men killed in action, and anticipated the fearful blow that would bring him down with a smash on the pavement. Instinctively he raised his left arm as if to shield his face. At length he reached safety, breathless and incredulous. Then he looked back. Half way across was Savrola, walking steadily and drawn up to his full height. Thirty yards away he stopped and, taking off his felt hat, waved it in defiance at the distant barricade. Tiro saw him start as he lifted his arm, and his hat fell to the ground. He did not pick it up, and in a moment was beside him, his face pale, his teeth set, every muscle rigid. "Now tell me," he said, "do you call that a hot fire?"

"You are mad," replied the Subaltern.

"Why, may I ask?"

"What is the use of throwing away your life, of waiting to taunt them?"

"Ah," he answered, much excited, "I waved my hat in the face of Fate, not at those wretched irresponsible animals. Now to the palace; perhaps we are already too late."

They hurried on through the deserted streets with the sound of musketry growing ever louder, and mingling with it now the shouts and yells of a crowd. As they approached the scene they passed through groups of people, peaceful citizens for the most part, anxiously looking towards the tumult. Several glanced fiercely at the soldier whose uniform made him conspicuous; but many took off their hats to Savrola. A long string of stretchers, each with a pale, shattered figure on it, passed by, filing slowly away from the fight. The press became thicker, and arms were now to be seen on all sides. Mutinous soldiers still in their uniforms, workmen in blouses, others in the dress of the National Militia, and all wearing the red sash of the revolt, filled the street. But Savrola's name had spread before him and the crowd divided, with cheers, to give him passage.

Suddenly the firing in front ceased, and for a space there was silence, followed by a ragged spluttering volley and a low roar from many throats.

"It's all over," said the Subaltern.

"Faster!" cried Savrola.

CHAPTER XX.

THE END OF THE QUARREL.

About a quarter of an hour after Lieutenant Tiro had escaped along the telegraph-wires, the attack on the palace was renewed with vigour. It seemed, moreover, that the rebels had found a new leader, for they displayed considerable combination in their

104

tactics. The firing increased on all sides. Then, under cover of their musketry, the enemy debouched simultaneously from several streets, and, rushing down the great avenue, delivered a general assault. The garrison fired steadily and with effect, but there were not enough bullets to stop the advancing crowds. Many fell, but the rest pressed on impetuously and found shelter under the wall of the courtyard. The defenders, realising they could no longer hold this outer line of defence, fell back to the building itself, where they maintained themselves among the great pillars of the entrance, and for some time held the enemy's fire in check by shooting accurately at all those who put their heads over the wall or exposed themselves. Gradually, however, the rebels, by their great numbers, gained the supremacy in the fire-fight, and the defenders in their turn found it dangerous to show themselves to shoot.

The musketry of the attack grew heavier, while that of the defence dwindled. The assailants now occupied the whole of the outer wall, and at length completely silenced the fire of the surviving adherents of the Government. Twenty rifles were discharged at any head that showed; yet they showed a prudent respect for these determined men, and gave no chances away. Under cover of their fire, and of the courtyard wall, they brought up the field-gun with which the gate had been broken in, and from a range of a hundred yards discharged it at the palace. The shell smashed through the masonry, and burst in the great hall. Another followed, passing almost completely through the building and exploding in the breakfast-room on the further side. The curtains, carpets, and chairs caught fire and began to burn briskly; it was evident that the defence of the palace was drawing to a close.

Sorrento, who had long schooled himself to look upon all events of war from a purely professional standpoint, and who boasted that the military operation he preferred above all others was the organising of a rearguard from a defeated army, felt that nothing further could be done. He approached the President.

Molara stood in the great hall where he had lived and ruled for five years with a bitter look of despair upon his face. The mosaic of the pavement was ripped and scored by the iron splinters of the shells; great fragments of the painted roof had fallen to the ground; the crimson curtains were smouldering; the broken glass of the windows lay on the floor, and heavy clouds of smoke were curling in from the further side of the palace. The President's figure and expression accorded well with the scene of ruin and destruction.

Sorrento saluted with much ceremony. He had only his military code to believe in, and he took firm hold of that. "Owing, Sir," he began officially, "to the rebels having brought a gun into action at close range, it is my duty to inform you that this place has now become untenable. It will be necessary to capture the gun by a charge, and expel the enemy from the courtyard."

The President knew what he meant; they should rush out and die fighting. The agony of the moment was intense; the actual dread of death was increased by the sting of unsatisfied revenge; he groaned aloud.

Suddenly a loud shout arose from the crowd. They had seen the smoke of the fire and knew that the end was at hand. "Molara, Molara, come out! Dictator," they cried, "come out or burn!"

It often happens that, when men are convinced that they have to die, a desire to bear themselves well and to leave life's stage with dignity conquers all other sensations. Molara remembered that, after all, he had lived famous among men. He had been almost a king. All the eyes of the world would be turned to the scene about to be enacted; distant countries would know, distant ages would reflect. It was worth while dying bravely, since die he must.

He called his last defenders around him. There were but thirty left, and of these some were wounded. "Gentlemen," he said, "you have been faithful to the end; I will demand no more sacrifices of you. My death may appease those wild beasts. I give you back your allegiance, and authorise you to surrender."

"Never!" said Sorrento.

"It is a military order, Sir," answered the President, and walked towards the door. He stepped through the shattered woodwork and out on the broad flight of steps. The courtyard was filled with the crowd. Molara advanced until he had descended half way; then he paused. "Here I am," he said. The crowd stared. For a moment he stood there in the bright sunlight. His dark blue uniform-coat, on which the star of Laurania and many orders and decorations of foreign countries glittered, was open, showing his white shirt beneath it. He was bare-headed and drew himself up to his full height. For a while there was silence.

Then from all parts of the courtyard, from the wall that overlooked it and even from the windows of the opposite houses, a ragged fusilade broke out. The President's head jerked forward, his legs shot from under him and he fell to the ground, quite limp. The body rolled down two or three steps and lay twitching feebly. A man in a dark suit of clothes, and who apparently exercised authority over the crowd, advanced towards it. Presently there was a single shot.

At the same moment Savrola and his companion, stepping through the broken gateway, entered the courtyard. The mob gave passage readily, but in a sullen and guilty silence.

"Keep close to me," said Savrola to the Subaltern. He walked straight towards the steps which were not as yet invaded by the rebel soldiery. The officers among the pillars had, with the cessation of the firing, begun to show themselves; someone waved a handkerchief.

"Gentlemen," cried Savrola in a loud voice, "I call upon you to surrender. Your lives shall be spared."

Sorrento stepped forward. "By the orders of His Excellency I surrender the palace and the Government troops who have defended it. I do so on a promise that their lives shall be safe."

"Certainly," said Savrola. "Where is the President?" Sorrento pointed to the other side of the steps. Savrola turned and walked towards the spot.

106

Antonio Molara, sometime President of the Republic of Laurania, lay on the three lowest steps of the entrance of his palace, head downwards; a few yards away in a ring stood the people he had ruled. A man in a black suit was reloading his revolver; it was Karl Kreutze, the Number One of the Secret Society. The President had bled profusely from several bullet-wounds in the body, but it was evident that the coup de grâce had been administered by a shot in the head. The back and left side of the skull behind the ear was blown away, and the force of the explosion, probably at close quarters, had cracked all the bones of the face so that as the skin was whole, it looked like broken china in a sponge bag.

Savrola stopped aghast. He looked at the crowd, and they shrank from his eye; gradually they shuffled back, leaving the sombre-clad man alone face to face with the great Democrat. A profound hush overspread the whole mass of men. "Who has committed this murder?" he asked in low hoarse tones, fixing his glance on the head of the Secret Society.

"It is not a murder," replied the man doggedly; "it is an execution."

"By whose authority?"

"In the name of the Society."

When Savrola had seen the body of his enemy, he was stricken with horror, but at the same time a dreadful joy convulsed his heart; the barrier was now removed. He struggled to repress the feeling, and of the struggle anger was born. Kreutze's words infuriated him. A sense of maddening irritation shook his whole system. All this must fall on his name; what would Europe think, what would the world say? Remorse, shame, pity, and the wicked joy he tried to crush, all fused into reckless ungovernable passion. "Vile scum!" he cried, and stepping down he slashed the other across the face with his cane.

The man sprang at his throat on the sudden impulse of intense pain. But Lieutenant Tiro had drawn his sword; with a strong arm and a hearty good will he met him with all the sweep of a downward cut, and rolled him on the ground.

The spring was released, and the fury of the populace broke out. A loud shout arose. Great as was Savrola's reputation among the Revolutionaries, these men had known other and inferior leaders more intimately. Karl Kreutze was a man of the people. His socialistic writings had been widely read; as the head of the Secret Society he had certain assured influences to support him, and he had conducted the latter part of the attack on the palace. Now he had been destroyed before their eyes by one of the hated officers. The crowd surged forward shouting in savage anger.

Savrola sprang backwards up the steps. "Citizens, listen to me!" he cried. "You have won a victory; do not disgrace it. Your valour and patriotism have triumphed; do not forget that it is for our ancient Constitution that you have fought." He was interrupted by shouts and jeers.

"What have I done?" he rejoined. "As much as any here. I too have risked my life in the great cause. Is there a man here that has a wound? Let him stand forth, for we are comrades." And for the first time, with a proud gesture, he lifted his left arm. Tiro perceived the reason of the start he had given when running the gauntlet in Constitution Square. The sleeve of his coat was torn and soaked with blood; the linen of his shirt protruded crimson; his fingers were stiff and smeared all over.

The impression produced was tremendous. The mob, to whom the dramatic always appeals with peculiar force, were also swayed by that sympathy which all men feel for those injured in a common danger. A revulsion took place. A cheer, faint, at first, but growing louder, rose; others outside the courtyard, ignorant of the reason, took it up. Savrola continued.

"Our State, freed from tyranny, must start fair and unsullied. Those who have usurped undue authority, not derived from the people, shall be punished, whether they be presidents or citizens. These military officers must come before the judges of the Republic and answer for their actions. A free trial is the right of all Lauranians. Comrades, much has been done, but we have not finished yet. We have exalted Liberty; it remains to preserve her. These officers shall be lodged in prison; for you there is other work. The ships are coming back; it is not yet time to put away the rifles. Who is there will see the matter through,—to the end?"

A man, with a bloodstained bandage round his head, stepped forward. "We are comrades," he cried; "shake hands."

Savrola gripped him. He was one of the subordinate officers in the rebel army, a simple honest man whom Savrola had known slightly for several months. "I entrust a high duty to you. Conduct these officers and soldiers to the State Prison; I will send full instructions by a mounted messenger. Where can you find an escort?" There was no lack of volunteers. "To the Prison then, and remember that the faith of the Republic depends on their safety. Forward, Gentlemen," he added, turning to the surviving defenders of the palace; "your lives are safe, upon my honour."

"The honour of a conspirator," sneered Sorrento.

"As you like, Sir, but obey."

The party, Tiro alone remaining with Savrola, moved off, surrounded and followed by many of the crowd. While they did so a dull heavy boom came up from the sea-front; another and another followed in quick succession. The fleet had returned at last.

CHAPTER XXI.

THE RETURN OF THE FLEET.

Admiral de Mello had been true to his word, and had obeyed the order which had reached him through the proper channel. He was within a hundred miles of Port Said when the despatch-boat, with the Agent of the Republic, had been met. He at once changed his course, and steamed towards the city he had so lately left. His fleet consisted of two battleships, which, though slow and out of date, were yet formidable machines, two cruisers, and a gunboat. The inopportune bursting of a steam-pipe on board the flagship, the Fortuna, caused a delay of several hours, and it was not till two o'clock in the afternoon of the second day that he rounded the point and saw the harbour and city of Laurania rise fair and white on the starboard bow. His officers scanned the capital, which was their home and of whose glories they were proud, with anxious eyes; nor were their fears unfounded. The smoke of half a dozen conflagrations rose from among the streets and gardens; the foreign shipping had moved out of the basin and lay off in the roads, for the most part under steam; a strange red flag flew from the fort at the end of the mole.

The Admiral, signalling for half-speed, picked his way towards the mouth of the channel cautiously. It was so contrived that a vessel in passing must be exposed to a cross-fire from the heavy guns in the batteries. The actual passage was nearly a mile wide, but the navigable channel itself was dangerously narrow and extremely difficult. De Mello, who knew every foot of it, led the way in the Fortuna; the two cruisers, Sorato and Petrarch, followed; the gunboat Rienzi was next, and the other battleship, Saldanho, brought up the rear. The signal was made to clear for action; the men were beat to quarters; the officers went to their posts, and the fleet, assisted by a favourable tide, steamed slowly towards the entrance.

The rebel gunners wasted no time in formalities. As the Fortuna came into the line of fire, two great bulges of smoke sprang from the embrasures; the nine-inch guns of the seaward battery were discharged. Both shells flew high and roared through the masts of the warship, who increased her speed to seven knots and stood on her course followed by her consorts. As each gun of the forts came to bear, it was fired, but the aim was bad, and the projectiles ricochetted merrily over the water, raising great fountains of spray, and it was not until the leading ship had arrived at the entrance of the channel, that she was struck.

A heavy shell, charged with a high explosive, crashed into the port-battery of the Fortuna, killing and wounding nearly sixty men, as well as dismounting two out of the four guns. This roused the huge machine; the forward turret revolved and, turning swiftly towards the fort, brought its great twin guns to bear. Their discharge was almost simultaneous, and the whole ship staggered with the violence of the recoil. Both shells struck the fort and exploded on impact, smashing the masonry to splinters and throwing heaps of earth into the air; but the harm done was slight. Safe in their bomb-proofs, the rebel gunners were exposed only to the danger of missiles entering the embrasures; while such guns as fired from barbette mountings were visible only at the moment of discharge.

Nevertheless the great ship began literally to spout flame in all directions, and her numerous quick-firing guns searched for the embrasures, sprinkling their small shells with prodigal rapidity. Several of these penetrated, and the rebels began to lose men. As the ships advanced, the cross-fire grew hotter, and each in succession replied furiously. The cannonade became tremendous, the loud explosions of the heavy guns being almost drowned by the incessant rattle of the quick firers; the waters of the harbour were spotted all over with great spouts of foam, while the clear air showed the white smoke-puffs of the bursting shells. The main battery of the Fortuna was completely silenced. A second shell had exploded with a horrid slaughter, and the surviving sailors had fled from the scene to the armoured parts of the vessel; nor could their officers induce them to return to that fearful shambles, where the fragments of their comrades lay crushed between masses of senseless iron. The sides of the ships were scored and torn all over, and the copious streams of water from the scuppers attested the energy of the pumps. The funnel of the Fortuna had been shot off almost level with the deck, and the clouds of black smoke floating across her quarters drove the gunners from the stern-turret and from the after-guns. Broken, dismantled, crowded with dead and dying, her vitals were still uninjured, and her captain, in the conning tower, feeling that she still answered the helm, rejoiced in his good fortune and held on his course.

The cruiser Petrarch had her steam steering-gear twisted and jammed by a shell, and becoming unmanageable grounded on a sand-bank. The forts, redoubling their fire, began to smash her to pieces. She displayed a white flag and stopped firing: but of this no notice was taken, and as the other ships dared not risk going ashore in helping her, she became a wreck and blew up at three o'clock with a prodigious report.

The Saldanho, who suffered least and was very heavily armoured, contrived to shelter the gunboat a good deal, and the whole fleet passed the batteries after forty minutes' fighting and with a loss of two hundred and twenty men killed and wounded, exclusive of the entire crew of the Petrarch, who were all destroyed. The rebel loss was about seventy, and the damage done to the forts was slight. But it was now the turn of the sailors. The city of Laurania was at their mercy.

The Admiral brought his ships to anchor five hundred yards from the shore. He hoisted a flag of truce, and as all his boats had been smashed in running the gauntlet, he signalled to the Custom-House that he was anxious for a parley, and desired that an officer should be sent.

After about an hour's delay, a launch put out from the jetty and ran alongside the Fortuna. Two rebel officers in the uniform of the Republican Militia, and with red sashes round their waists, came on board. De Mello received them on his battered quarter-deck, with extreme politeness. Rough sailor as he was, he had mixed with men of many lands, and his manners were invariably improved by the proximity of danger or the consciousness of power. "May I ask," he said, "to what we are indebted for this welcome to our native city?"

The senior of the two officers replied that the forts had not fired till they were fired upon. The Admiral did not argue the point, but asked what had happened in the city. On hearing of the Revolution and of the death of the President, he was deeply moved. Like Sorrento, he had known Molara for many years, and he was an honest, open-hearted man. The officers continued that the Provisional Government would accept his surrender and that of his ships, and would admit him and his officers to honourable terms as prisoners of war. He produced the authorisation of the Committee of Public Safety, signed by Savrola.

De Mello somewhat scornfully requested him to be serious.

The officer pointed out that the fleet in its battered condition could not again run the gauntlet of the batteries and would be starved out.

To this De Mello replied that the forts at the head of the harbour were in like condition, as his guns now commanded both the approaches by the military mole and the promontory. He also stated that he had six weeks' provisions on board and added that he thought he had sufficient ammunition.

His advantage was not denied. "Undoubtedly, Sir," said the officer, "it is in your power to render great services to the Provisional Government and to the cause of Liberty and Justice."

"At present," replied the Admiral dryly, "it is the cause of Justice that appears to need my support."

To that the officers could find no more to say than that they had fought for a free Parliament and meant to have their way.

The Admiral took a turn or two before replying. "My terms are these," he said at last. "The leader of the conspiracy—this man, Savrola—must be surrendered at once and stand his trial for murder and rebellion. Until this has been done, I will not treat. Unless this is done by six o'clock to-morrow morning, I shall bombard the town and shall continue to do so until my terms are complied with."

Both officers protested that this would be a barbarity, and hinted that he would be made to answer for his shells. The Admiral declined to discuss the matter or to consider other terms. As it was impossible to move him, the officers returned to the shore in their launch. It was now four o'clock.

As soon as this ultimatum was reported to the Committee of Public Safety at the Mayoralty, something very like consternation ensued. The idea of a bombardment was repugnant to the fat burgesses who had joined the party of revolt so soon as it had become obvious that it was the winning side. It was also distasteful to the Socialists who, however much they might approve of the application of dynamite to others, did not themselves relish the idea of a personal acquaintance with high explosives.

The officers related their interview and the Admiral's demands.

"And if we refuse to comply?" inquired Savrola.

"Then he will open fire at six o'clock to-morrow morning."

"Well, Gentlemen, we shall have to grin and bear it. They will not dare to shoot away all their ammunition, and so soon as they see that we are determined, they will give in. Women and children will be safe in the cellars, and it may be possible to bring some of the guns of the forts to bear on the harbour." There was no enthusiasm. "It will be an expensive game of bluff," he added.

"There is a cheaper way," said a Socialist delegate from the end of the table, significantly.

"What do you propose?" asked Savrola looking hard at him; the man had been a close ally of Kreutze.

"I say that it would be cheaper if the leader of the revolt were to sacrifice himself for the sake of Society."

"That is your opinion; I will take the sense of the Committee on it." There were cries of "No! No!" and "Shame!" from many present. Some were silent; but it was evident that Savrola had the majority. "Very well," he said acidly; "the Committee of Public Safety do not propose to adopt the honourable member's suggestion. He is overruled,"—here he looked hard at the man, who blenched,—"as he will frequently be among people of civilised habits."

Another man got up from the end of the long table. "Look here," he said roughly; "if our city is at their mercy, we have hostages. We have thirty of these popinjays who fought us this morning; let us send and tell the Admiral that we shall shoot one for every shell he fires."

There was a murmur of assent. Many approved of the proposal, because they thought that it need never be carried into execution, and all wanted to prevent the shells. Savrola's plan, however wise, was painful. It was evident that the new suggestion was a popular one.

"It is out of the question," said Savrola.

"Why?" asked several voices.

"Because, Sirs, these officers surrendered to terms, and because the Republic does not butcher innocent men."

"Let us divide upon it," said the man.

"I protest against a division. This is not a matter of debate or of opinion; it is a matter of right and wrong."

"Nevertheless I am for voting."

"And I," "And I," "And I," shouted many voices.

The voting went forward. Renos supported Savrola on legal grounds; the case of the officers was now sub judice, so he said. Godoy abstained. The majority in favour of the proposal was twenty-one to seventeen.

The count of hands was received with cheering. Savrola shrugged his shoulders. "It is impossible that this can go on. Are we become barbarians in a morning?"

"There is an alternative," said Kreutze's friend.

"There is, Sir; an alternative that I should gladly embrace before this new plan was carried out. But," in a low menacing tone, "the people will be invited to pronounce an opinion first, and I may have an opportunity of showing them their real enemies and mine."

The man made no reply to the obvious threat; like all the others he stood in considerable awe of Savrola's power with the mob and of his strong dominating character. The silence was broken by Godoy, who said that the matter had been settled by the Committee. A note was therefore drafted and despatched to the Admiral, informing him that the military prisoners would be shot should he bombard the city. After further discussion the Committee broke up.

Savrola remained behind, watching the members move slowly away talking as they went. Then he rose and entered the small room he had used as his office. His spirits were low. Slight as it was, his wound hurt him; but worse than that, he was conscious that there were hostile influences at work; he was losing his hold over the Party. While victory was still in the balance he had been indispensable; now they were prepared to go on alone. He thought of all he had gone through that day; the terrible scene of the night, the excitement and anxiety while the fighting was going on, the strange experience in the square, and, last of all, this grave matter. His mind, however, was made up. He knew enough of De Mello to guess what his answer would be. "They are soldiers," he would say; "they must give their lives if necessary. No prisoner should allow his friends to be compromised on his account. They should not have surrendered." When the bombardment began he could imagine fear turning to cruelty, and the crowd carrying out the threat that their leaders had made. Whatever happened, the affair could not be allowed to continue.

He rang the bell. "Ask the Secretary to come here," he said to the attendant. The man departed, and in a few moments returned with Miguel. "What officer has charge of the prison?"

"I don't think the officials have been altered; they have taken no part in the Revolution."

"Well, write an order to the Governor to send the prisoners of war, the military officers taken this afternoon, in closed carriages to the railway station. They must be there at ten o'clock to-night."

"Are you going to release them?" asked Miguel opening his eyes.

"I am going to send them to a place of security," answered Savrola ambiguously.

Miguel began to write the order without further comment. Savrola took the telephone off the table and rang up the railway-station. "Tell the traffic-manager to come and speak to me. Are you there?—The President of the Executive Committee of the Council of Public Safety—do you hear? Have a special train,—accommodation for thirty—ready to start at ten p.m. Clear the line to the frontier,—yes,—right to the frontier."

Miguel looked up from his writing quickly, but said nothing. Although he had deserted the President when he saw that he was ruined and his cause lost, he hated Savrola with a genuine hatred. An idea came into his head.

CHAPTER XXII.

LIFE'S COMPENSATIONS.

Much had happened, though but a few hours had passed since Savrola left his house to hurry to the Mayoralty. The deep and intricate conspiracy, which had been growing silently and in secret for so many months, had burst on the world's stage and electrified the nations. All Europe had learned with amazement of the sudden and terrible convulsion that in a few hours had overthrown the Government which had existed for five years in Laurania. In the fighting that had raged throughout the ninth of September upwards of fourteen hundred persons had been killed and wounded. The damage done to property had been enormous. The Senate-House was in flames; the palace had been destroyed; both, together with many shops and private houses, had been looted by the mob and the mutineers. Fires were still smouldering in several parts of the city; in many homes there were empty places and weeping women; in the streets the ambulances and municipal carts were collecting the corpses. It had been a momentous day in the annals of the State.

And all through the terrible hours Lucile had waited, listening to the sound of the musketry, which, sometimes distant and fitful, sometimes near and sustained, suggested the voice of a wrathful giant, now sunk in sulky grumblings, now raised in loud invective. She had listened in sorrow and suspense, till it was lost in the appalling din of the cannonade. At intervals, between the bathos of the material consolations of the old nurse,—soup, custards, and the like—she had prayed. Until four o'clock, when she had received a message from Savrola acquainting her with the tragedy at the palace, she had not dared to add a name to her appeals; but thenceforward she implored a merciful Providence to save the life of the man she loved. Molara she did not mourn: terrible and cruel as was his death, she could not feel she had suffered loss; but the idea that he had been killed on her account filled her heart with a dreadful fear of guilt. If that were so, she said to herself, one barrier was removed only to be replaced by another. But the psychologist might cynically aver that force and death were the only obstacles that would restrain her affection for Savrola, for above all she prayed for his return, that she might not be left alone in the world.

Her love seemed all that was left to her now, but with it life was more real and strongly coloured than in the cold days at the palace amid splendour, power, and admiration. She had found what she had lacked, and so had he. With her it was as if the rising sunbeam had struck the rainbow from the crystal prism, or flushed the snow peak with rose, orange, and violet. With Savrola, in the fierce glow of love the steady blue-white fires of ambition had become invisible. The human soul is subjected to many refining agents in the world's crucible. He was sensible of a change of mood and thought; no longer would he wave his hat at Fate; to his courage he had now added caution. From the moment when he had seen that poor, hideous figure lying on the steps of the palace, he had felt the influence of other forces in his life. Other interests, other hopes, other aspirations had entered his mind. He searched for different ideals and a new standard of happiness.

Very worn and very weary he made his way to his rooms. The strain of the preceding twenty-four hours had been tremendous, and the anxieties which he felt for the future were keen. The step he had taken in overruling the Council and sending the prisoners into foreign territory was one the results of which he could not quite estimate. It was, he was convinced, the only course; and for the consequences he did not greatly care, so far as he himself was concerned. He thought of Moret,—poor, brave, impetuous Moret, who would have set the world right in a day. The loss of such a friend had been a severe one to him, privately and politically. Death had removed the only disinterested man, the only one on whom he could lean in the hour of need. A sense of weariness, of disgust with struggling, of desire for peace filled his soul. The object for which he had toiled so long was now nearly attained and it seemed of little worth, of little comparative worth, that is to say, beside Lucile.

As a Revolutionist he had long made such arrangements with his property as to make sure of a competence in another land, if he had to fly Laurania; and a strong wish to leave that scene of strife and carnage and to live with the beautiful woman who loved him took possession of his mind. It was, however, his first duty to establish a government in the place of that he had overthrown. Yet when he reflected on the cross-grained delegates, the mean pandering crowd of office-seekers, the weak, distrustful, timid colleagues, he hardly felt that he cared to try; so great was the change that a few hours had worked in this determined and aspiring man.

Lucile rose to meet him as he entered. Fate had indeed driven them together, for she had no other hope in life, nor was there anyone to whom she could turn for help. Yet she looked at him with terror.

His quick mind guessed her doubt. "I tried to save him," he said; "but I was too late, though I was wounded in taking a short cut there."

She saw his bandaged arm, and looked at him with love. "Do you despise me very much?" she asked.

"No," he replied; "I would not marry a goddess."

"Nor I," she said, "a philosopher."

Then they kissed each other, and thenceforward their relationship was simple.

But in spite of the labours of the day Savrola had no time for rest. There was much to do, and, like all men who have to work at a terrible pressure for a short period, he fell back on the resources of medicine. He went to a little cabinet in the corner of the room and poured himself out a potent drug, something that would dispense with sleep and give him fresh energy and endurance. Then he sat down and began to write orders and instructions and to sign the pile of papers he had brought with him from the Mayoralty. Lucile, seeing him thus employed, betook herself to her room.

It was about one o'clock in the morning when there came a ringing at the bell. Savrola, mindful of the old nurse, ran down and opened the door himself. Tiro, in plain clothes, entered. "I have come to warn you," he said.

"Of what?"

"Someone has informed the Council that you have released the prisoners. They have summoned an urgency meeting. Do you think you can hold them?"

"The devil!" said Savrola pensively. Then after a pause he added, "I will go and join them."

"There are stages laid by road to the frontier," said the Subaltern. "The President made me arrange them in case he should wish to send Her Excellency away. If you decide to give up the game you can escape by these; they will hold them to my warrant."

"No," said Savrola. "It is good of you to think of it; but I have saved this people from tyranny and must now try to save them from themselves."

"You have saved the lives of my brother-officers," said the boy; "you can count on me."

Savrola looked at him and an idea struck him. "These relays were ordered to convey Her Excellency to neutral territory; they had better be so used. Will you conduct her?"

"Is she in this house?" inquired the Subaltern.

"Yes," said Savrola bluntly.

Tiro laughed; he was not in the least scandalised. "I am beginning to learn more politics every day," he said.

"You wrong me," said Savrola; "but will you do as I ask?"

"Certainly, when shall I start?"

"When can you?"

"I will bring the travelling-coach round in half-an-hour."

"Do," said Savrola. "I am grateful to you. We have been through several experiences together."

They shook hands warmly, and the Subaltern departed to get the carriage.

Savrola went up-stairs and, knocking at Lucile's door, informed her of the plan. She implored him to come with her.

"Indeed I wish I could," he said; "I am sick of this; but I owe it to them to see it out. Power has little more attraction for me. I will come as soon as things are settled, and we can then be married and live happily ever afterwards."

But neither his cynical chaff nor arguments prevailed. She threw her arms round his neck and begged him not to desert her. It was a sore trial. At last with an aching heart he tore himself away, put on his hat and coat, and started for the Mayoralty.

The distance was about three quarters of a mile. He had accomplished about half of this when he met a patrol of the rebel forces under an officer. They called on him to halt. He pulled his hat down over his eyes, not wishing for the moment to be recognised. The officer stepped forward. It was the wounded man to whom Savrola had entrusted the escorting of the prisoners after the surrender of the palace.

"How far are we away from the Plaza San Marco?" he asked in a loud voice.

"It is there," said Savrola pointing. "Twenty-third Street is the number."

The rebel knew him at once. "March on," he said to his men, and the patrol moved off. "Sir," he added to Savrola, in the low, quick voice of a man in moments of resolve, "I have a warrant from the Council for your arrest. They will deliver you to the Admiral. Fly, while there is time. I will take my men by a roundabout way, which will give you twenty minutes. Fly; it may cost me dear, but we are comrades; you said so." He touched Savrola's wounded arm. Then louder to the patrol: "Turn down that street to the right: we had better get out of the main thoroughfare; he may sneak off by some lane or other." Then again to Savrola: "There are others coming, do not delay;" and with that he hurried after his men. Savrola paused for a moment. To go on was imprisonment, perhaps death; to return, meant safety and Lucile. Had it been the preceding day, he would have seen the matter out; but his nerves had been strained for many hours,—and nothing stood between them now. He turned and hurried back to his house.

The travelling-coach stood at the door. The Subaltern had helped Lucile, weeping, into it. Savrola called to him. "I have decided to go," he said.

"Capital!" replied Tiro. "Leave these pigs to cut each other's throats; they will come to their senses presently."

So they started, and as they toiled up the long ascent of the hills behind the city, it became daylight.

117

"Miguel denounced you," said the Subaltern; "I heard it at the Mayoralty. I told you he would let you in. You must try and get quits with him some day."

"I never waste revenge on such creatures," replied Savrola; "they are their own damnation."

At the top of the hill the carriage stopped, to let the panting horses get their wind. Savrola opened the door and stepped out. Four miles off, and it seemed far below him, lay the city he had left. Great columns of smoke rose from the conflagrations and hung, a huge black cloud in the still clear air of the dawn. Beneath the long rows of white houses could be seen the ruins of the Senate, the gardens, and the waters of the harbour. The warships lay in the basin, their guns trained upon the town. The picture was a terrible one; to this pass had the once beautiful city been reduced.

A puff of white smoke sprang from a distant ironclad, and after a while the dull boom of a heavy gun was heard. Savrola took out his watch; it was six o'clock; the Admiral had kept his appointment with scrupulous punctuality. The forts, many of whose guns had been moved during the night to the landward side, began to reply to the fire of the ships, and the cannonade became general. The smoke of other burning houses rose slowly to join the black, overhanging cloud against which the bursting shells showed white with yellow flashes.

"And that," said Savrola after prolonged contemplation, "is my life's work."

A gentle hand touched his arm. He turned and saw Lucile standing by him. He looked at her in all her beauty, and felt that after all he had not lived in vain.

Those who care to further follow the annals of the Republic of Laurania may read how, after the tumults had subsided, the hearts of the people turned again to the illustrious exile who had won them freedom, and whom they had deserted in the hour of victory. They may, scoffing at the fickleness of men, read of the return of Savrola and his beautiful consort, to the ancient city he had loved so well. They may learn how Lieutenant Tiro was decorated for his valour in the war with the little bronze Lauranian Cross which is respected all over the world; of how he led the Lancers' polo team to England according to his desire, and defeated the Amalgamated Millionaires in the final match for the Open Cup; of how he served the Republic faithfully with honour and success and rose at last to the command of the army. Of the old nurse, indeed, they will read no more, for history does not concern itself with such. But they may observe that Godoy and Renos both filled offices in the State suited to their talents, and that Savrola bore no malice to Miguel, who continued to enjoy good-fortune as a compensation for his mean and odious character.

But the chronicler, finding few great events, other than the opening of colleges, railways, and canals, to recount, will remember the splendid sentence of Gibbon, that history is "little more than the register of the crimes, follies, and misfortunes of mankind"; and he will rejoice that, after many troubles, peace and prosperity came back to the Republic of Laurania.

Made in the USA
Monee, IL
03 January 2024

51036914R00069